BITTER WORMWOOD

BITTER WORMWOOD

EASTERINE KIRE

ZUBAAN
is an imprint of Kali for Women
Zubaan
128b Shahpur Jat
1st floor
New Delhi 110 049
www.zubaanbooks.com

First published by Zubaan, 2011
Copyright © Easterine Kire, 2011

ISBN: 978 93 81017 02 9

Zubaan is an independent feminist publishing house based in New Delhi,
India, with a strong academic and general list. It was set up as an imprint of
the well known feminist house Kali for Women and carries forward Kali's
tradition publishing world quality books to high editiorial and production
standards. "Zubaan" means tongue, voice, language, speech in Hindustani.
Zubaan is a non-profit publisher, working in the areas of the humanities
social sciences, as well as in fiction, general non-fiction, and books for
young adults that celebrate difference, diversity and equality, especially for
and about the children of India and South Asia under its imprint Young
Zubaan.

Typeset by Jojy Philip, New Delhi 110 015
Printed at Raj Press, R-3 Inderpuri, New Delhi 110 012

AUTHOR'S INTRODUCTION

The struggle for independence from India by the Naga people, indigenous inhabitants of the Naga Hills, has been a story hidden for several decades. Cleverly concealed by censorship on newspaper reports, there was only one western journalist, a British war correspondent named Gavin Young (*The Daily Telegraph*) who managed to enter Nagaland illegally in the 1960s and report what he saw of the genocide and rape and torture of the Nagas by the Indian Army.

The IWGIA (International Work Group for Indigenous Affairs) 1986 report *The Naga Nation and its Struggle against Genocide*, recorded that as many as 100,000 Nagas were killed in fighting with India beginning from 1956. Naga Federal government statistics claim that villagers who fled their burnt villages and died of starvation and disease bring the number closer to 200,000 from the 50s to the 60s. The main source of information for the IWGIA report was Naga historian Dr. Visier Sanyu.

The first killings occurred in 1948 when two Nagas were shot dead by the Indian army in Tuensang, followed by another two killings in 1950, and the attack on Khonoma village and Lungkhum village in 1953. In 1954, the numbers rose to 64 Nagas killed and at the beginning of 1955, 279 Nagas were recorded killed by the army. Between January 1955 and July 1957 the estimated damage stood at: 79,794 houses burnt, 26,550,000 mounds of paddy burnt and 9,60,000,000 rupees worth of goods destroyed (source: *The Naga Chronicle* pp. 148 and 181).

The IWGIA report documents some of the tortures in April and May 1955 by the Assam Police Battalion, beginning with the burning of 200 granaries of Mokokchung village. This was accompanied by atrocities like beating a pregnant woman and forcing her to give birth in public, raping of the village women and killing of the menfolk. In September the harvest was destroyed by the same police battalion and five village women were raped, amongst whom were two minor girls. Both young students and adults were shot and killed or tortured to death by the battalion.

In 1956, the Indian army began taking prisoners and using them for target practice. Groupings of villagers and tortures of the villagers became routine by 1957. The stories of torture documented by both the IWGIA and *The Naga Chronicle* seem to surpass each other in the army's inhuman treatment of the Nagas: men were tied to poles and burned; they were buried alive; their genitals were given electric currents. Each instance of torture was more gruesome and horrible than the next. The report lists the tortures and repression of the Nagas by the Indian army as "i) execution in public; ii) mass raping; iii) deforming sex organs; iv) mutilating limbs and body;

v) electric shocks; vi) puncturing eyes; vii) hanging people upside down; viii) putting people in smoke-filled rooms; ix) burning down of villlages; x) concentration camps; xi) forced starvation and labour." One of the stories of rape had as its intention the desecration of the village church of Yankeli where four minor girls were raped by the Maratha contingent on 11 July, 1971. The church building was abandoned by the villagers after that incident.

Of the reports, one of the most pitiable incidents occured in 1962. The village of Matikhru was attacked by the Indian army and all the women and children were chased out of the village. After that all the male adults were tortured and beheaded. This was followed by the burning of the village. The village holds an annual Remembrance day when they re-enact the killing of the 12 male members of the village.

The conflict which began as a peaceful resistance of Indian occupation escalated into a violent full-scale war after the death of Mahatma Gandhi. Gandhiji had supported the Naga right to remain independent of India and even declared that anyone who tried to force them into the Indian Union would have to deal with him first. Sadly the Mahatma was killed in that first rush after independence and Nehru, the first Prime Minister of free India, chose the path of military aggression to make the Nagas submit.

At the height of military oppression in 1956, the Naga Army was formed and its members travelled to China and East Pakistan to find arms to fight the Indian army. Subsequent groups that went to China in the mid-70s were exposed to Chinese Marxist ideology. Factional killings begun by breakaway groups erupted in the Naga National Council in this period, eroding the Naga cause through the years.

In 1980, the first factional group called themselves the National Socialist Council of Nagaland and used the slogan, "Nagaland for Christ." After some years, there was a split in the NSCN, and two factional groups appeared, the Isak Muivah and the Khaplang factions. The factions began killing off the leaders of the Naga National Council, and drug addicts and drug peddlers, as well as members of their rival groups on a large scale right through the 80s, 90s and up till 2008. In the continuous infighting amongst the Naga freedom fighters, Naga society was riven apart by extortion, and rapid brutalization.

Today, many young Nagas struggle with a confused identity. This confusion began after India launched its war of occupation and enacted the creation of Naga statehood in 1963. Statehood was an agreement between a small group of Nagas and the Delhi government. Under statehood, Indian citizenship was imposed on Nagas, but they were denied many of the rights of citizens of India under the Indian constitution. Laws like the Armed Forces Special Powers Act and the Disturbed Areas Act took away the fundamental rights of Nagas and continued to put them at the mercy of the armed forces.

The situation in the Indian metropolises is worrying. Students and workers from the Northeast continue to face racist attacks. *The Times of India* dated October 27, 2009 carried a long article entitled, "Girls from NE soft target in city." It listed various incidents including the rape and murder of a 6-year-old girl from the Northeast, the murder of a Naga girl by an IIT student and the beating up of Naga and a number of Northeast people by locals. Sexual harassment and rape of Naga girls were initially denied redressal by the police in Indian cities but by 2009, the Ministry DonNER had decided to set "North-East Connect" to provide relief to beleaguered students (*Assam Tribune*, Oct 30, 2009).

The North East Support and Help Centre (NESHC), a very crucial helpline begun in September 2007, recorded that 86 percent of people from the Northeast had experienced racist attacks. Shortly after the murder of the Naga girl, *The Times of India* carried two more reports on November 7 and November 9, 2009 on the beating up of two Naga students and the molestation of a Naga girl. The bitterness and suspicion between the mainland Indians and Nagas in Indian cities easily triggers new conflicts contributing to the alienation.

In Nagaland, Christian groups and civil society groups such as the Naga Mothers Association, Naga Hoho, Naga Baptist Church Council, the Gaonbura and Dobashi association, Naga Students Federation and Naga Christian Fellowship have vainly tried time and again to bring the warring Naga groups to reconcile with each other. However, in 2009, all the peace efforts seemed to be making some headway. The State Police recorded a total of 12 factional killings as contrasted with a total of 300 in the previous years (source: Comparative Crime Statistics for the year 2006, 2007, 2008 up to 15th December, 2009. Nagaland Police) give the source of the statistics.

With killings on the decline and the active efforts of the Forum for Naga Reconciliation (FNR) group, there seems to be a flickering light in the horizon. The Nagas are hopeful that the quest for lasting peace in these long-troubled, tear-sodden hills of home was in sight. The Reconciliation team is made up of apex tribal bodies and organizations and has been very active for the last 36 months of its life. Led by

Dr Wati Aier, the FNR brought the NSCN(IM) and the NSCN(K) to sign a "Covenant of Reconciliation" declaration where both parties promised to pursue Naga reconciliation and forgiveness.

Though there have been a few hiccups, the Forum is still maintaining course and has found support from the International Baptist World Alliance which consists of 120 nations. The BWA which met in Kuala Lumpur in July 2011 passed a resolution supporting the Naga reconciliation process (report carried in *The Morung Express* July 9, 2011). The FNR's appeal to the Naga public makes the search for peace a community responsibility.

This book is not meant to be read as a history textbook. For the purpose of reading about the history of the Naga struggle, researchers should read comprehensive books on the topic for example, *The Naga Chronicle*, *The Naga Saga*, *Nagaland File* and *Naga Identities* and *The Naga Resistance*. This book is not about the leaders and heroes of the Naga struggle. It is about the ordinary people whose lives were completely overturned by the freedom struggle. Because the conflict is not more important than the people who are its victims.

Easterine Kire
September 2011

2007

"Get out of the way, old man!" a hand roughly pushed Mose aside. The owner of the hand then made his way through the gasping crowd. Actually, the terrified crowd had swiftly begun to scatter at his approach, and the killer, holding out his pistol, effortlessly strode out onto the main street. There were no policemen in sight. The killer made his way toward the Dak Lane side-street. Then he began to quicken his pace. All that anyone could hear for a long time was the sound of running feet.

It was over quickly. The young man who was shot lay dead in a spreading pool of blood. Shops quickly downed their shutters. Vegetable-sellers trying to save their goods scampered off with their baskets of vegetables.

After some minutes, there were just a few people left in the crowded market. Mose stayed rooted to the spot, but when everything became quiet, he crept over to look at the body. One of the shots had gone wild. Luckily it was embedded in the wall of a hotel. No one else had been harmed. There had been times when bystanders had been injured, even killed by stray shots in these shootings.

Mose looked down at the body on the ground. The dead man was no longer twitching. Blood-red tomatoes lay crushed under his feet, and vegetables dropped by frightened shoppers were strewn on the ground near him. Sand clung to his mouth from which a small trickle of blood had begun to flow. The blood-spill from his chest was steadily spreading on the ground. He was very young. He looked barely twenty. In death, it was difficult to tell which tribe he belonged to. Short cropped hair, smart clothes and expensive shoes.

Mose noted all these facts quickly, before the police came and unceremoniously dumped the body into a van and rushed it to the morgue. The standard routine was to take the victims of shootings to the emergency unit of the hospital. But it was obvious that there was nothing that could be done for the young man. Once the van had driven off and a police cordon established round the area, Mose turned towards home. He was still clutching the plastic bag in which he had been carrying the chillies and brinjals he had bought just before the shooting.

The streets were deserted now. House-owners had hastily locked their doors and faces peered out from behind curtains in windows. The deathly stillness of yet another day brought to a close by a sudden killing brooded over the town. Tomorrow life would begin again slowly, cautiously. For tonight however, even the foolhardy would stay indoors, talking in hushed tones about the killing.

There was no curfew on, but the town was very still. Though there were lights in the windows of the crowded houses along the streets, there was hardly any movement on the streets. Only the occasional police car cruising past.

Mose walked out of the Supermarket area past the shuttered

shops. The smell of rotting vegetables assailed his nostrils as he crossed the alley that led to the Dak Lane road. There were two stray dogs on the road, looking for scraps of food. Mose slowed down when he reached the beginning of the steep Mission road. Again, all the shops on either side of the road were closed. It was amazing how quickly news of a shooting could spread.

The old wooden houses on the Mission road leaned against each other in the twilight. Most of the wooden houses in this hill town were being replaced by concrete structures these days. When he reached the Choto Bosti road he walked faster. At the turning houses were built halfway down the slope. Below the last house were fields and then the river. Mose stayed on the main road and headed towards Seikhazou. He caught up with a neighbour and they continued on their way home.

"They're too late," muttered the neighbour as a white police gypsy went past.

"You're right," Mose agreed. "The killers are too smart. In any case, no one dares to catch them."

"Everyone is afraid of them. That's a fact," the neighbour stated.

"Everyone is sick of it, all these killings But no one has the guts to do anything about it," was Mose's reply.

"No," said the neighbour. "Maybe if we had guns too." They both knew it was a lame idea.

Mose and his neighbour walked on silently. At the next turning, they parted ways. Mose's house was further on. He walked slowly. He wasn't in a hurry. He felt he needed the time to think over things. The almost daily killings, the young men on the streets calloused by hate and shouting at everyone in sight and the complete collapse of cultural life – it was unbelievable that it could come to this, thought Mose.

The war that they'd begun with India more than 60 years ago was a just war. The Nagas had been fighting against the takeover of their ancestral lands by the new nation of India. Men readily came forward to replace those fallen in ambushes and encounters. Villagers fled into the forests and many died of starvation. But the survivors were tenacious and had fought on. In all the villages they had entered they had been hailed as heroes, soldiers of the Naga army who the villagers never grudged sharing their meagre food supplies with. He had felt so proud to be a soldier back then, a freedom fighter. But now, these killings, this terrorising of their own people – was this what it had come to? Mose checked himself as a sob rose in his throat. No, not that way, he would not shed tears again.

He felt helpless as he turned at the bamboo crossing and headed up the path to his house. He had built the two-storyed brick house himself. Mose opened the gate and entered the small yard, relieved to have reached home safely. But his thoughts stayed on the incident in town. What was it the killer had shouted? Old man. Mose felt he could still hold a gun as well as any other and sprint so that none could overtake him. Old man. Those words came back painfully to him.

"Mose!" his wife's voice woke him out of his reverie. "Man, are you mad? Didn't you know we would be worried about you?" she scolded loudly as she took the bag from him.

"There was a shooting in town," Mose began.

"Do you think we don't know it?" his wife snapped. "I was about to send Vila to look for you. When will you remember you are an old man now? Think how awful it would be for me if you were shot?"

Mose's wife was a big woman and quite strong willed. He cringed as he realized he would not hear the end of this harangue. So he stated quietly,

"I was not anywhere near them." He didn't say anything beyond that. Dissatisfied, his wife kept scolding and upbraiding him for the inconvenience he had caused to members of his family by being out during a shooting. Finally Mose said, "Enough, woman. I have not died today." She heard the tense anger in his voice and stopped her tirade then.

That was how it was between them these days, icy silences and things left unsaid. He sometimes felt his life was passing him by, particularly when he found himself wandering alone aimlessly in the town or neighbourhood. But outside his home, Mose continued to be a respected elder in the community. Young men sought him out to listen to his stories. His peers desired his counsel when it came to land disputes and other clan disputes. He still had admirers of his fairness and life wisdom.

Mose sat down heavily on the porch. Kohima town lay spread out in front of him on the opposite side of the valley. Each house was bright with lights. Stars filled the sky, spread thickly over the forested hills surrounding the large township. He could hear the frogs croaking from the stream below his house. He also heard another voice. Old man, Mose heard that voice over and over again. Like a harsh reprimand. Old man, the young killer had hissed. Old man, shouted his wife when he came home. Old man, repeated the voices in his head.

Mose didn't feel old. For a moment back there, the blood

had rushed to his head when he had heard the younger man rasp out at him. He had almost charged him. He knew exactly what tackle to use to disarm him. If he had dared to stop the young man, he might have held him off temporarily but not for long for there was no real strength left in his arms. And what would have followed? He would have become just another statistic. There had been a deadness in the killer's eyes as he glared at Mose. These were men for whom life and death were just games.

It had not begun like that. The freedom struggle that Mose had been a part of, the struggle that the dead-eyed young man of today claimed to be a part of, had not always been like that. Memories flooded Mose's mind as he sat out on the porch. No, it had not been like that at all.

PART ONE

BIRTH

Mose was born in 1937. No one knew the date but it was in late September just as the fields were being readied to be harvested. His mother, Vilaü, was in the fields, tying together the stalks of rice that would be harvested the following week. Suddenly she felt cramping pains low in her abdomen. She tried to continue working, but the pains came again and intensified. Their field was an hour and a half away from the village, so the young mother birthed her son in the field shed.

Vilaü's mother-in-law, Khrienuo, helped her to wash the infant with a little water from the stream. Then she sent her daughter-in-law home with her infant son wrapped in a little bundle of cloth. No further ceremony to it. Khrienuo stayed on a bit to finish the rest of the work. Their neighbours were not surprised when they saw Vilaü walking past their fields with the baby. Women birthing while out in the fields was not an uncommon phenomenon in those days.

Vilaü bathed her baby properly once she had reached home. She made sure to remove all traces of mucus from his mouth and nose as she had been taught. The midwife had heard the baby's cries. She came running.

"*Hou*, Vilanuo, you should not have gone to the field today," she lightly admonished the young mother,

"Didn't you have any dreams last night?"

"I did but I thought it would be in the evening," replied Vilaü. "I really needed to get the paddy ready for the harvest. Besides, I did not have my pains until late in the morning, by which time I was already at work."

"Oh well, you'll just have to be more alert next time," said the midwife, as she placed the baby on her lap to examine him.

"How thick his hair is!" she exclaimed as she continued her examination. "Look at that forehead! Ohh...this one is going to be a warrior one day, I can just tell."

"Oh, *Anyie*, how can you tell?" asked Vilaü.

"Look at that wide forehead!It means he is going to wield a spear."

"Or a gun," said his mother thoughtfully.

The midwife insisted that Vilaü should go to bed. She then began to cook the evening meal. The baby was restless now and pushed away with his tongue, the water that Vilaü was feeding him. He made little cries of complaint.

"That is a hungry cry, he needs milk, try and feed him," said the midwife. Vilaü clumsily offered her breast and he began to feed voraciously.

"See? If you pay attention you will know when he is asking for food, or wanting to sleep or be changed. Babies are not very complicated." Vilaü smiled at the midwife and quietly fed her baby.

Anyie: maternal aunt

"You should think of a name for him soon. I am sure your mother-in-law, Khrienuo, will have thought of something by now. Our people always name our children as soon as they can, because naming them makes them members of the clan and protects them from being taken by spirits."

"Oh really? I didn't know it protected them from the spirits."

"Knowledge of these things comes slowly, with life, with experience," said the midwife with a smile.

The chicken broth was soon ready. She served her two cupfuls of the rich soup in a deep tin bowl.

"Drink as much as you can of the soup," she said to Vilaü. "It helps your body to make more milk."

Vilaü ate well as she was quite hungry after the birthing. She was tired too and lay back after eating her fill.

Khrienuo came home soon after and the midwife left saying, "You are in safe hands now."

That evening, Khrienuo had a name for the child. "We will call him Moselie, it means one-who-will-meet-life-without-guile. It is a good name. It means that he will never plot to harm another person."

"It's an unusual name, Mother. I have never heard it before," said Vilaü thoughtfully. "It's a good name, I like it," she added.

The two women spent the next days caring for the baby. Khrienuo was a widow. She had been widowed for ten years now. She lived in the house adjoining theirs and they jointly owned the fields. Vilaü's husband, Luo-o, was very pleased their first child was a boy. He happily took over the task of harvesting the field so his wife did not have to return to field-work in the next month. It was quite usual for new mothers to strap their babies on their backs and work at the fields. Harvest-time was such a crucial time and if there was a sudden storm the grain could fall off the stalks and be lost. People worked faster in the harvesting week. Vilaü was grateful to be spared the hard labour as her baby was growing rapidly and seemed to want feeding very frequently.

THE TREE RITUAL

Luo-o was a proud father. He liked to carry his son around the village square. Moselie was a healthy baby. Everyone called him Mose and the name stuck. At seven months he was crawling on the mud floor of his parents' house. He always needed careful watching because he had a habit of picking up small objects from the floor, and trying to eat them. The months passed quickly and he was soon waddling behind his mother. She carried him to the fields and back, but kept him close to her as she worked in the water-logged fields in raintime. The toddler could play all day in the fields and was none the worse for it.

"*Hou*! what a strong constitution he has!" remarked his grandmother, Khrienuo. This pleased his mother greatly.

"He has never been sick, not even for a day," Vilaü said proudly. "Remember when he had a little fever at eight months? That was just because he was teething and after that he has never been sick."

"Good, may he soon be blest with siblings," Khrienuo said and smiled. Both knew that child-bearing women were expected to have more children within a gap of two years or one and a half years.

Mose had now begun to say his first words. "Ta, Ta," he called out to his grandmother whenever he saw her. He had shortened the word Atsa for grandmother to Ta. Khrienuo would proudly pick him up and give him a treat. She liked to carry him round the village in the evening and he would point out to old women and call out "Ta, Ta." People enjoyed seeing the two of them together for Mose was a happy child, smiling happily when anyone approached them. For a week or two, the only word he spoke was, "Ta" but in the next weeks he quickly followed it up with his own names for his parents.

Luo-o now spent more time with the men of his age-group. They were planning a festival to celebrate a new gate for the clan. This would be a whole tree, ritually selected and cut and dragged from the forest with a great deal of ceremony.

"The seer has shown us the exact tree," he explained to his wife and mother. "It is deep in the forest but there are no other big trees nearby so it will be easy enough to find it."

"Where is it, son?" Khrienuo asked.

"Towards Dzübo, it is about a four hour walk from here, so we will be gone two days."

"Be careful, son, those are areas which used to be known as unclean regions in the old days."

"We will be careful, Mother. The seer warned us too."

"Hmm, has he had any bad dreams?" Khrienuo questioned.

"He didn't say anything. However, he warned us thrice to be careful. But the clan badly needs a new gate. I'm sure it will be all right. There are twenty of us. We will find the tree and cut it down after the elder has done the neccesary rituals. Then we will come home on the second day. It will be the duty of the whole clan to drag it home."

"Well son, when a seer gives a warning, no one should take it lightly," said his mother.

"We will be careful," Luo-o promised.

On the morning of his departure, Luo-o was restless and impatient. He tore about the house looking for his dao-holder and when he had found it, he put it on hastily and bid his wife and son a quick farewell.

The party returned the same evening but not before one of their clansmen had run ahead with the sad news. Luo-o had been crushed by the tree when they were felling it. He had died instantly. The tree was abandoned, even though it had been ritually selected, because it was taboo to use it after it had claimed a life. Vilaü screamed at the news. Her screams brought Khrienuo running and shouting, "No! Not Luo-o, let it not be true!"

But it was only too true and the wailing of the two women alerted the rest of the clan to the tragedy that had struck them.

After Luo-o's burial, the household was hushed by this sudden invasion of death and even the young Mose seemed to sense that something was very wrong. He wandered around the house and called, "Apfu, Apfu." Vilaü did not know what to tell him in the beginning, and she would burst out crying. The little boy began to associate his questions with the sadness of his mother and stopped asking after some time.

Vilaü mourned her husband for years. It made her alternate in her treatment of her young son. Some days she let him do as he wished. On other days she was quite harsh with him.

She rarely smiled now. Her clanspeople saw her beside her husband's grave frequently, weeping.

Luo-o's death had hit his family very hard indeed. Khrienuo was just as grieved as Vilaü by the loss of her only son, but she took it more wisely. She had had her share of losses in life. She said to those close to her: "If life is hard to you, you simply harden yourself so its griefs are easier to bear. That is the only way to meet it."

Khrienuo was very loving to her grandson. She saw the bitterness in her daughter-in-law and knew it would take a long time to heal. She tried to compensate for it by giving young Mose more of her time, and cooking meals for them as often as she could. Vilaü was not an insensitive woman. She saw these efforts made by her mother-in-law and was grateful. In the first year, Mose seemed to prefer staying at his grandmother's house. The boy sensed the dismal atmosphere in his own house.

At his grandmother's he played happily with his mud pellets and tried to shoot them out of a small slingshot. Khrienuo would laughingly teach him to place a pellet in the middle of the slingshot, and pull it back so that the pellet shot out. He would manage a shot or two, but would cry if he had let go of the rubber too fast and it slammed back and hit his finger painfully. "Bad, bad sling," he would shout and throw the slingshot away and run crying to his grandmother. But in minutes he would have forgotten the pain and picked up the slingshot again to try and master it.

"THE JAPANESE ARE COMING!"

Mose turned five in 1942. He had made friends with a neighbour's son, Neituo, who was the same age as he. The two became inseparable. Most mornings Mose would run out of the house and be at Neituo's house as soon as his friend woke up.

"Come back soon, food's nearly ready," his mother would shout after him. But she knew she would have to go across half an hour later to bring him back to eat the morning meal. Vilaü let him go, knowing that he would be well behaved at other people's houses, never eating their food and saying the right things at the right time. Neighbours often complimented her on her son's good manners. She had taught him well. She and Khrienuo had decided that he was ready for school the next year, but when 1943 came, the war closed down the schools in Kohima.

Along with their clanspeople, Mose, his mother and grandmother fled the Japanese invasion of their village. Their small family sought refuge in the village of Rukhroma.

They were given an abandoned house to stay in and the villagers shared their food with them. Mose could only hazily recollect this period of his life. When the area where they were sheltering in was shelled, they left the village. His maternal uncle had carried him on his back, and they had trekked several jungle paths and camped in the woods. He had one vivid memory of seeing a war plane crash with a deafening sound into some rocks at Zubza. It was such an exciting sight for him and he had wished they would see more planes crashing.

By the time the war was over and the schools reopened, Mose was seven. A quiet boy, he was the smallest in his class at the Mission School. Mose liked school and was a quick learner which pleased his teachers a lot. "This boy will go far," predicted one of the male teachers.

Mose was always accompanied by Neituo. Of the two, Mose was the more diligent. Neituo was not unintelligent but he was lazy. School seemed tedious to him after the initial excitement of the first two months rubbed off. There were ten of them in the first class. Four girls and six boys. Their teacher was strict with them, but gave them sweets if they had learnt their alphabets and numbers. The missionary who ran the school was also very strict. Mose was in awe of him. The older students often went to his house to run errands after school. They spoke confidently to him in English. Mose understood only snatches of what they said. He dearly wished to speak as they did.

"School over!" he declared in English when he came home in the afternoon. As he said it, he flung his bag on the mud floor of their house. It made his mother and grandmother laugh out loud.

"Oh, so now we shall all speak in English to each other, shall we?" his grandmother asked.

"Yes," Mose answered with a big smile.

"What is your name?" Khrienuo asked her grandson in English.

"Grandmother! You never told me you could speak English!" Mose burst out in Tenyidie.

"Well, you never asked me before," Khrienuo responded with a smile.

"Mother, how about you? Did you ever learn to speak English?" Mose wanted to know.

"No, I had no time for that nonsense," Vilaü replied. "There was no school when I was young."

"Well, how did Grandmother learn it then?" the boy asked.

"Uh, ha ha," Khrienuo laughed, "when the men got drunk they could all speak English, and that is what I picked up. Our neighbours would come home drunk on Saturday nights and two of them would always get into a fight because one would ask, "What is your name?" and the other would reply, "*No tokai!*" The one asking would not give up and in the end they would be so angry that they would go at each other with their fists. Before we learnt what it meant, we thought the question was a very offensive one. But it was not that, it was actually their drunkenness that led to their quarreling over such an innocent question."

They all laughed at this story. Khrienuo explained to Mose,

Tenyidie: language spoken by the seven tribes of the Tenyimia, Mose's community.

No tokai: meaning not allowed, slang used by young boys

"The two of them had worked with the white soldiers as labourers so they picked up some English words from that time. That was how most of the men learnt English."

"Now show us what you have learned at school today," said his mother.

Mose happily unpacked his schoolbag and laid out his drawings. The two women praised his drawings of animals and people. In his other notebook, he had written down his alphabets in big letters.

"Can you read that to us?" asked his mother, "Your grandmother and I could learn English from you!"

Mose laughed at the thought that he might someday teach his mother and grandmother. He pictured the two of them sitting in small chairs like the ones they sat on at school and trying to write on the small tables in front.

"You'd never fit into the chairs," he protested.

"What do you mean, son?" asked his mother.

"If you went to school to learn English, you would be too big to sit in our chairs," he explained.

"Oh that?" said his grandmother, "We would bring our own chairs to school."

The boy smiled at that idea.

Mose was soon distracted when their neighbour's cat slipped into their kitchen.

"Drat that cat, must be trying to steal meat again," Vilaü said. The boy sprang up after the cat and chased it out the door. In turn, the cat ran into the chickens outside, so there was an almighty racket with the hens squawking and the cat mewling as it raced off.

The two women looked at each other and smiled. They were so proud of the boy. Khrienuo and Vilaü continued to live alongside each other's houses. It was a good arrangement because Mose could be babysat by his grandmother if Vilaü needed to attend a funeral or help at a festival. Most nights the three of them ate together, but the women were wise enough to maintain their separate kitchens. "Sharing a hearth breaks up a friendship," the elders used to say.

NEW THINGS

In 1947, Mose proudly went to the third grade having passed his exams. Neituo had scraped through so the two were still together. The school was moved to a new location, the former hospital in town. Many new houses were being built since the war had destroyed most of the houses. The thatch houses became a thing of the past and only tin roofs could be seen. It was a longer walk for the two boys, but they were bigger now. Mose was nearly ten and Neituo was nine months older. They walked to school on their own, very proud that they were able to go to school unescorted.

Meanwhile, Vilaü worked at the fields alone. The hardest work was the ploughing of the new fields in January and February before the rains set in. The wintry ground was stony. Though she was a good worker, Vilaü felt that it needed a man to dig up the iron earth. She worked slowly, having learned to pace herself at this sort of work.

Each day she took a new section and, before the end of the day, she went back and beat on the overturned earth with the back of her hoe. That kept the earth from hardening completely. Sometimes, a shower would fall in January and that was very welcome. It softened the soil and made labour easier the next day. When Mose was grown he would help her, she encouraged herself with this thought. Widowhood was hard because the woman had to till the fields alone. Certainly she received some help from her in-laws and male relatives but being a young widow, Vilaü wanted to finish as much as she could on her own.

"Leave some for us, Vilaü," Beilie called out, Luo-o's cousin, as he walked past her field.

"Don't worry, there will be plenty left," she answered. Beilie had five children aged 3 to 12. He and his wife tilled a much bigger field. Vilaü was aware of all this and did not want to add to his burden. Her own brother had six children. She couldn't expect much help from him.

This year they were all using the new grain popularly called rosholha, the grain distributed by the British government after the war. Those who had some stores of native seed-grain continued to use it. However, people with big families preferred rosholha, which yielded more grain than native grain. It was easier to cultivate and it was a more sturdy plant that withstood heavy rain better.

In the afternoon, Vilaü rested in the shade of the small shed and surveyed her labour of the morning. It wasn't enough. Digging was back-breaking work and Vilaü had learned to take it slowly, resting periodically. That helped her to work more effectively. Her mother-in-law was visiting relatives at another village today, so she was quite alone in the fields. The wind carried the voices of her neighbours over to her. But when they died down, all she could hear was a solitary bird crying for its mate.

Later, when the sun was setting, she heard the voices of her neighbours again as they got ready to go home. She rose to wash herself at the stream and join them. When all of them converged at the field path, they were a group of seven people. Beilie and his wife and son, and Vilaü and three more adults. They joked a bit. Beilie said, "We should think of something less laborious to plant than rice."

"Ah, yes, why don't we all learn to eat roti and bread?" asked the neighbour.

"Indeed," Beilie responded, "it must be easier to grow wheat than rice. Why did we have to choose such a diet?"

All of them laughed at this. It was unthinkable that they would stop cultivating rice.

"In America, they use only tractors I'm told. None of this hard digging with hoes," said the neighbour.

"We could all buy one together," Beilie stated.

They all laughed again at the idea of themselves getting a tractor to their hilly fields.

They went on in this vein until they reached the village. Mose was waiting for his mother by the wayside and he tried to help her with her basket, but she said it was all right and refused to give it to him.

The two of them bid the others goodnight and walked homeward.

"When is Grandmother returning?" asked Mose.

"Tomorrow evening. She said she wouldn't be gone long. She doesn't like to stay away for long."

"Good. I miss her cooking" said Mose. "School's closed tomorrow so I can help you in the field," he added.

"That is nice, son. I need all the help I can get and you can learn more of field-work. What holiday is that?"

"It's Saturday, Mother, we never have school on Saturdays, remember?"

Vilaü smiled.

"Ah, your genna-day, then," she said.

"What is a genna-day Mother?"

"Well, it is a day when no one works or goes to the fields. We do that to please the spirits."

"What would happen if we worked on a genna-day?"

"Something disastrous. People fear to break a taboo because it always ends badly."

"Well, Saturday is not exactly a genna-day."

"No, it isn't."

When their evening meal was over, they sat by the fireplace and exchanged their news. "Mother, can we buy a radio?" asked Mose suddenly.

"Why? What do we need a radio for?" asked his mother.

"The teacher said we should all listen to the radio. Every day. At school, they make us listen to the radio in one of the classes. We learn about other countries and what is happening there. Today, there was a man on the radio saying that the white man will soon leave and go back to England."

"*Hou!* Then who will be the government if the white man goes away?" exclaimed his mother.

"I don't know. What about our men? They all work with the white man. Surely some of them will know how to run the government without him?"

"We have never had a government without the white man. I don't think any of our men know enough. Anyway, tell me more about the radio. Did your teacher tell you how much it might cost?"

"About 25 rupees," replied Mose.

"That is a lot of money," said Vilaü slowly, "I will have to see."

A SQUIRREL FOR DINNER

The next morning, Mother and son went to the fields. It was so early that they could see the dew on the short grass. Mist was rising from the fields as they hurriedly made a fire to warm the kettle of water. A movement in the bushes made Mose reach for his slingshot. A large squirrel ran into the undergrowth and was climbing up a tree. Mose took aim and shot at it. The pellet hit the squirrel on the head and Mose saw it fall. Springing after it, he proudly brought it to his mother.

"Ah, you've already done a man's work. That will make a nice dinner. Your grandmother will be so proud of you. We will cook it and wait for her."

The squirrel was as big as a small cat. Vilaü cut a young cane into strips. Then she thrust one through the squirrel's neck and strung it up on the wall of the shed.

"That should keep it safe from thieves," she said as she hung it up.

They then went to the field and began to dig the soil. Mose

anxiously ran back to the shed thrice to see if the squirrel was still there.

"*Hou*! why don't you tie it to your waistband and keep on working?" said his mother in exasperation. After that remonstration, Mose stopped running back and forth.

Mose was using a smaller hoe than his mother's. Vilaü taught him to dig in patches. That way, he could see how much work he had done in the course of the day. They had seven plots that they regularly cultivated. Two of the plots were big and the other five were of average size. They were now working on the first of the big plots. The smaller plots were on a slope, while the biggest plots were at the bottom of the valley. In this area everyone cultivated terrace fields. It was more laborious than jhum fields, the slash-and-burn method. Nevertheless people preferred terrace fields which did not damage the soil as jhumming did.

"How much rice can we grow here, Mother?" he asked.

"About eight tins, it's a lot."

"And how much in the other plots? The small plots?"

"Oh about three in each, I would say," his mother responded.

Mose began to count on his fingers, "Eight, sixteen, nineteen, twenty-two, twenty-five, twenty- eight...Mother we eat twenty-eight tins of rice in a year!"

Vilaü stood upright and laughed at her son.

"We eat more than that, son. This field gives us food only for seven or eight months. But your grandmother gives us some paddy as well. That is how we survive."

After that little exchange, they worked on the field again until they were both very hungry.

"Time to eat, son," Vilaü said as she carefully placed her

hoe in the ground with the blade facing inward. Mose did the same and they washed their hands at the small stream.

When she served him food, Mose ate hungrily and rapidly.

"Eat slowly son, food stays longer in your stomach if you eat slowly."

"But I am so hungry now, Mother. I just want to eat everything I see."

"Now you see why we have to work so hard to grow rice," said his mother.

After lunch, it was back to the field again. But they did not work as hard as in the morning.

"People work best in the morning. That's what my mother used to say. That's why I was delaying our lunch hour," she explained to her son.

"That's funny. They should actually work better after eating."

"True, but the body grows sluggish after food."

The two worked on desultorily and stopped for a little break. Mose had struck a stone with his hoe and almost cut his foot on the sharp edge. Only the top of it was visible. Vilaü felt for the stone with her hand, dug a bit and soon dislodged the stone. It was double the size of her fist and one of the edges was very sharp. "*Hou*! Son, if you had cut your foot on that it would have gone deep!" she showed the stone to Mose and he hurled it into the woods.

"Next time, line it up against the border of the fields. That way we will have a nice rocky border for our field," said Vilaü.

She then remembered that her mother-in-law would be home by now.

"That stone must be a signal for us to stop working," she said to her son.

"Can we go home and cook the squirrel for Grandmother now?" Mose asked eagerly.

"We shall do that. I can work again the day after. Any blisters on your hands?" she asked.

Mose examined his palm closely.

"None today, Mother," he said proudly.

"Oh, you must be getting a worker's hands," said his mother. Vilaü's hands were calloused from years of working the fields.

The two washed themselves at the stream and placed their belongings in Vilaü's basket and made their way home.

Close to the village they could see smoke rising from Khrienuo's house.

"Grandmother's home, I can see smoke from her house," said Mose happily.

"Let's hope she hasn't started to cook yet."

Mose began to run at that. Calling out and stumbling a bit, he burst into his grandmother's house.

"Don't cook yet Grandmother, don't cook till you see what I have for you!"

He thrust the squirrel into his grandmother's hand, startling her.

"What is that?" she almost shrieked.

"I shot it, Grandmother. It's a big squirrel, can you cook it?"

"Of course I will, my child," she said quickly recovering herself and remembering to add, "Oh, you are so clever! And you must tell me how you shot it. Squirrel meat is very good for you."

Khrienuo found a long bamboo with a spiked end. She thrust it through the squirrel and began to roast it on the flames.

"Can we eat it like that, Grandmother?" Mose asked excitedly.

"Ha ha, of course not, it needs to be quartered and cooked for at least an hour. I know you like the smell of roasted meat, but it is not fit for eating like that."

Vilaü, entering the kitchen, began to look for ginger to pound.

"Can you believe that he got that before we started working? It was as though it was waiting for him."

Khrienuo made the appropriate responses and Mose felt very proud of himself.

"Can you pound some garlic too, Vilanuo?"

"Why garlic Mother? Isn't ginger enough?"

"Squirrel tastes best with garlic, ginger and tree tomato," Khrienuo said decisively.

"Oh, I never knew that," Vilaü replied, hastening to find garlic cloves.

THE RADIO

After dinner, they talked about the radio and Vilaü said she had decided to buy one.

"Oh, shall we be listening to the little people inside?" Khrienuo asked with a smile.

When the radio first came to Kohima village, some people said that there were some little people inside the box who sang songs and read the news.

"Yes, and we could try singing in it ourselves," Vilaü added with a smile.

"Mother and Grandmother, surely you don't believe that anymore?" Mose asked with a little surprise.

"Sure I do," his grandmother continued, "why don't we open it? Just to make sure, you know?"

The following Saturday, Vilaü took Mose to town and the two of them bought a small transistor. It cost 22 rupees. Mose tested it in the shop and they bought four batteries as well. On the street, when there was no-one about, Mose played the radio a couple of times. His mother shushed him at first, but when he turned it on accidentally, they both looked at each other conspiratorially. Vilaü was just as excited as her son and once they were home, they quickly turned the knob on. A man's voice said something loudly in English. "What is he saying, son?" asked Vilaü.

"Wait, let me listen," said Mose and he put up the volume higher and stood listening very carefully.

"The departing British government has left behind two new nations, India and Burma. Partition is the new word that has been formed by the collapse of the British South Asian empire. India and Pakistan are being divided into two separate nations...." the man's voice droned on the radio.

Mose could not understand all of what the man said, but what he could, he explained carefully to his mother.

"What a marvellous thing it is!" Vilaü said, running her hand over the radio.

The two of them kept turning the knobs. They first listened to some songs and then to more news broadcasts. There were about four channels they could listen to. One was a Chinese station where a woman spoke very rapidly in Chinese. Mother and son laughed uproariously at that because they couldn't understand a word of what she was saying. Even the static made them giggle. Eventually, they made a habit of tuning the radio into the station where news was broadcast in English.

Mose wrote down words he didn't understand. Big words like repatriation, intermediary and resettlement. Even words that he knew but was a little unsure of like partition and nationalisation. He would ask his teachers because they always liked it when the students made an effort to learn new words on their own.

"Now I can learn English from the radio," Vilaü stated with a smile.

"Make sure it is English and not Chinese," Mose responded.

The radio became part of their evening ritual. After their supper, they turned on the radio for news at six pm. Khrienuo joined them as often as she could, quietly listening with the other two. On the first two evenings, both women interrupted the listening to ask Mose questions when they heard familiar words like India or Britain. "*Shie*! what is he saying about India?" Khrienuo had asked but the interruption distracted Mose from catching the rest of the sentence. He shushed them. After that, they learned to sit quietly through the news broadcast until Mose had absorbed it all. Then he would translate it to them.

"How big is America?" Vilaü asked, after they had listened to some news on the American elections.

"Wait, I will bring my atlas and we can see," Mose was almost shouting as he ran off to get it.

When they had spread out the map of North America, Khrienuo said, "Hmm, doesn't look very big, does it? Where's the map of India? Have you got that?"

Mose turned the pages until he found the Indian sub-continent.

"Nah, that's not big either," Khrienuo repeated, unconvinced.

"Grandmother, look at this portion which says Uttar Pradesh. If you tried, you could fit in Kohima a hundred times over into Uttar Pradesh. Does that tell you how big India is? How big the rest of the world is?"

"*Yha*!" Khrienuo exclaimed in awe, "I would never have thought of that. How clever you are my child, it was a good thing to send you to school. Your mother and I are getting educated as well, you should tell your teachers that."

"I'll do that, Grandmother. You could come to school and take an exam too."

"Yes, of course, we will come bringing our own chairs."

"And the radio," added his mother.

GANDHI, MARBLES AND
A PROPHECY

They had a good harvest that year. Mose diligently counted 33 tins of paddy.

"It's the work you put in. That's why we have a bigger harvest," said Vilaü.

"Really Mother? Have you never harvested so much before?"

"Only when your father was alive. We easily got 45 or 48 tins then, sometimes even 50. You are becoming a man, my son. You are bringing in a man's share."

"Not yet, Mother, it is a much smaller amount than Father's."

"But you are only ten. All right, nearly eleven. Think how much you could do if you turned fifteen."

Mose was very pleased at his mother's words. He wanted to be able to do so much more.

A great deal had happened in the year that was about to end. The British had left India and the radio was full of the news of the partition of India. After August 15, there were many reports of Muslims killed in India and Hindus killed in Pakistan. Vilaü and Khrienuo thought it was madness that people would kill their own neighbours. Mose picked up tidbits of news about it on the streets on his way to school and back. Men talked about it endlessly and he overheard certain phrases. 'Naga Independence' was one of the phrases he had heard. It stuck with him for the next many days. He mentioned it to Neituo at school.

"What did they mean by that?" asked Mose.

"Father says there is a group of people asking to be separate from India," replied Neituo.

"Well, that shouldn't be hard, should it?" Mose asked.

"Father was also saying that the group has gone to meet Gandhi. They will tell him that the Nagas want their own nation."

"Oh, then it will be all right. Gandhi is a kind man, isn't he? I'm sure he will agree to it."

"Gandhi is a good man, yes. Everyone says that."

The two soon lost interest in the subject when they heard the bell ring for recess. "I've got five new marbles," Neituo said in a low whisper. They ran out to a spot behind the class room. There were smooth spots on the ground with small scooped-out holes for marble games. This was a favourite area for the younger boys who played out quick games before running back to class after recess. The two of them played with two new marbles. The old ones were cracked in places and did not roll well. The boys had their own lucky marbles which they always carried around. Neituo's was a green one and Mose had a blue marble, a bit bigger in size than the others.

"Where's your daguli?" Neituo asked. That was how they referred to the marble each one kept as a lucky marble.

"I've got it with me but it's got a new crack," Mose answered.

"Get another one, then," said Neituo.

"If I get a new one, I'll have to try it out first and be quite sure I can use it as a daguli before I throw away the old one."

Marbles were confiscated daily at school but the boys continued to sneakily play their games. Once in a while a male teacher would come out and catch the players and confiscate all their marbles. Mose had seen a bucketful of marbles in the teachers' room.

"Bet they take them for their kids," he told Neituo.

"Yes, must be fun to be a teacher, and take away other people's stuff all the time."

When the bell rang, they scrambled to collect their marbles and spring back to class. The Maths teacher gave them a sidelong glance as they ran in. He was very strict with them.

"Humph, I should start doing sums with marbles," he said loudly.

The boys did not dare look up at him, but sat quietly in their places and tried to concentrate on their lesson.

School would close for the winter in two weeks' time. They had not got their results yet. Neituo was nervous, but Mose was confident for he had done well. He looked forward to getting his mark-sheet, but hid his excitement from Neituo. His friend disliked studying and was not scoring good grades. After school, the pair raced out the door to play another game before they went home.

Mose was not in a hurry because no one would be home at this hour. When he got home, he put away his school things and ate some of the leftovers from the morning meal. What was the time? Should he make the fire or go to meet his mother? In the end, he decided to make the fire and boil the water. That would please his mother more. She used to say it was easy to start the evening meal if there was hot water ready. I'll make Mother teach me how to cook, thought Mose, then I can have meals ready after school for us. Men didn't do the cooking except at festivals where they cooked for the community in enormous pots, turning over huge chunks of meat at intervals.

Mose had learned early on to make a fire. He filled the kettle with water and placed it on the growing flames. Presently, he heard their neighbours' voices. But they sounded agitated.

"That woman!" Neituo's mother was saying loudly, "That prophetess never says anything good. She always prophesies war."

Mose strained to hear more but they were mumbling now. He knew who they were talking about. It was a woman from Kigwema village. Long before the Japanese invasion, she had pranced into the village square and prophesied that there would be, not one, but two wars in their land, each following the other. Neituo's mother surely was referring to her as there was no other prophetess as well known as that one. He would mention it to his mother.

She came in presently and put her basket on the floor.

"What a thoughtful boy you are! You have got the fire going and the water boiled!" said his mother in a very pleased voice. She was standing up and retying her hair in a knot.

"You had better teach me to cook too," said Mose.

"Why? That is not men's work. Your father never cooked."

"Mother, I don't mind doing women's work if it helps you a little. Besides no one is going to see."

Vilaü simply smiled at this suggestion.

After food, Mose remembered their neighbour's words and mentioned it to his mother.

"Ohh, the old prophetess. She is a strong one, that one. Everything she prophesies comes true. I would take her seriously."

"What did she mean by saying there would be another war?"

"I don't know, son, we have always had one war or the other, hope it won't be a long one when it comes."

"I don't remember the last one well at all."

"You were barely five. We were lucky it was not a long war."

AN UNFINISHED LIFE

In the winter holidays, Mose accompanied his mother to the fields. At the edge of the field, he plucked a bitter wormwood leaf and stuck it behind his ear.

"Grandmother says it keeps the spirits away. Well, actually she said that it kept away those bad spirits that caused you to do bad things," he said to his mother by way of explanation. She laughed, but plucked a leaf as well and placed it in her basket. It was common to rub it on cuts and insect bites.

There wasn't much work to do now. The boy enjoyed being outdoors. Occasionally they took a pumpkin home for their dinner. Mose always had his slingshot with him, but he had only gotten a couple of birds.

"That squirrel must have been a fluke," he said in a disappointed tone.

"Don't say that, son; never speak out such things without thinking. Not if you want to be a great hunter."

"Why Mother?" he asked.

"Because our words destroy or make our destiny. The wives of hunters say, 'We are not satiated with the food you brought. You must bring more.'"

"How odd!" said Mose, "It almost sounds rude."

"Yes, but it makes the men get more game when their women say that."

"We want to eat more meat!" Mose shouted.

"I shall say it when we are at home," said his mother, stifling a giggle.

On the days that they stayed in the village, Vilaü and Khrienuo dried the paddy and ran in and out shooing chickens away. They took turns pounding the paddy in the long mortar that stood inside Vilaü's house. Except for these activities, the winter months were not as hectic as the summer months. The days were shorter and colder. The winter vegetables needed regular watering, especially mustard leaves and garlic.

Every evening, they sat after dinner and religiously listened to the news on the radio. On the 30th January, when Mose turned on the radio, he immediately raised his hand, indicating that everyone should be quiet. He gasped as he listened to the news and put his ear close to the speaker. He then tried putting up the volume but there was a crackling sound as he did this, so he lowered it again. After the long broadcast, readings from the Hindu scriptures accompanied by the harmonium could be heard on the radio.

Mose sat down and stated, "Gandhi was shot dead today!"

"Who is that? Gandhi. Gandhi. Isn't that the old man who is the leader of the Indians?" Khrienuo asked.

Mose nodded yes.

"Why would anyone do that? He looks so harmless," Vilaü stated.

"The radio says that they have caught the killer. We were studying about Gandhi in school last year. They call him the Father of the nation. Our teacher said he was the man who brought Indian independence. How sad that he should be killed!"

"Who was it that shot him? A white soldier?" Vilaü asked.

"No, they say it was a Hindu. A brown man."

"His own countryman? That is terrible."

They were all quiet for some time.

"He is not the leader of India, is he? That is some other man, isn't it?" Vilaü wanted to know.

"No, he is not the Prime Minister of India. That is Nehru."

"Are they brothers?" Khrienuo asked.

"No of course not," was Mose's reply.

"Oh, I always thought they were brothers. At the big meetings, the men always use their names together – Nehru-Gandhi, Gandhi-Nehru, like that. Hmm, nothing good can come out of killing a good man. That is for sure."

A week after the assassination of Gandhi school reopened. At the assembly, the Headmaster talked briefly about Gandhi and his life. Then he added, "Before he died, this great man met a group of Nagas. He asked how he could help them. The men said they wanted independence from India. Gandhi told them they had every right to it. This was truly a great man who understood the rights of all human beings. Gandhi's death is a loss not only to India but to the Nagas and to the whole world." They stood in silence for two minutes and prayed for his soul. Everyone looked solemn as they did this.

In the new school year, Mose and Neituo had both been promoted to the fourth grade. At first, the students were shy with the new teacher but in a week's time they had grown almost as boisterous as the year before. Some of the weaker students had not passed. Though there were still ten of them, two were students who had failed in the fourth grade. Their class teacher was much stricter than the previous one had been. He insisted that they buy all their books within four days. They were not allowed to come to class if they did not have books.

Soon, Mose's class was learning to write essays on different subjects. The reason for the rapid progress in teaching was the stipend exam they would take at the end of the next year. Those who passed the exam would receive a stipend to help them with their school fees.

"What a lot to study! Don't your teachers think it's too much?" Vilaü asked when Mose was home.

He had sat for two hours poring over his books by the light of the lantern.

"No, Mother, this is what they learn in the fourth grade every year."

"If you ask me, it's a great deal for a small boy."

"I'm a big boy now, Mother, I'm eleven."

"That's right. Still, it seems a lot of work to me. I'm glad I never went to school."

"Oh, Mother!" Mose laughed.

EGGS FOR JISU

Mose came home proudly from school one afternoon. His mother was at home, weaving.

"Mother, I've been selected!" he said.

"Selected for what, son?" Vilaü asked.

"The exam, remember the big stipend exam? I told you about it before..."

"Oh that? Yes, what about it?"

"My teacher says I can sit the exam at the end of the year."

"Won't everybody do that exam?"

"No, not everyone, Mother. Neituo can't do it because he failed in Math."

"Oh, all right."

"Mother, if I pass the exam, I will get money to study. Then you don't have to pay my school fees. That will be so good."

"Oh son, let's hope you get it then."

The year seemed to fly by with Mose immersed in his books. Neituo felt all alone.

"Meet me after school for a game of marbles?" Neituo asked.

"Can't. I've to study," was Mose's reply.

"I have new marbles," said Neituo temptingly.

"I can't play until I have finished the sums the teacher gave us today."

"Humph. Study, study, study, that is all you ever do now. Teacher's pet," Neituo was petulant.

"I'm not doing it for my own sake. It's for Mother."

"Why? How's that?"

"It's so she won't have to work so hard for my school fees. You have a father, you won't understand."

Neituo felt quite ashamed after that. They had never talked about that before.

"Hey, it's fine with me. You study all you want, okay? Maybe I will join you."

They both laughed at that because Neituo hated studying.

At the end of the year, Mose passed the exam.

"We are proud of you, Mose," said his grandmother.

"If your father were here today, he would be so proud of you," his mother joined in.

"Thank you," said Mose, "I feel very happy that I will be earning some money toward my schooling. I can say that, can't I? It will be an earning, won't it?"

"Oh, certainly son, it is what you will earn with your own hard work," Vilaü replied.

"We have had a good year," Khrienuo said solemnly, "we should give thanks to our creator."

Khrienuo and Vilaü were both non-Christians, but Mose had begun to recite the Christian prayers he learned at school. When he was quite convinced that he wanted to worship the Christian God, a gentle conversion of the whole family took place.

"I shall take two eggs to the wood and leave it for your *Jisu*," said Khrienuo earnestly.

"He is your Jisu too now," said Mose.

"Well, you know him better than I do since you met him first, so I shall call him your Jisu for some time."

"All right, Grandmother, I'm sure he won't mind."

"Ah, you must remember we have never had a God before who was so close that we could call him by name."

"I understand, Grandmother."

They began to attend the church services in the village. The morning services were crowded, and Khrienuo and Vilaü sat at the back of the church imitating what the others did, standing or sitting down as they were bid to. If they made a mistake, they would cover their mouths with their body-cloths and giggle.

One Sunday morning, the pastor announced at the end of the service: "We need to pray for our land. The Indian government has taken Zapuphizo prisoner for saying that the Naga people want independence. Hard times are ahead of us. Please continue to pray in your homes for peace in our land."

After church, everyone was discussing what the pastor had said. Some people had more information about it. They said that Phizo was in jail in central India for writing letters to the British Parliament.

Later that day when they were at home, Khrienuo asked,

"Can it be such a bad thing to write to the white man's government? What did Phizo write about?"

Jisu: native name for Jesus

"They say he wrote asking that Nagas should not be made a part of India," Mose tried to explain.

"Well, that is quite right. We have never been a part of India before. Why should we join them now?" Khrienuo asked.

"Yes, why should we join them?" Mose echoed.

"We should ask your Jisu to get Phizo out of jail soon. His children must miss him so much."

SHADOWS GATHERING

In 1950, Mose passed grade six. There was no doubt now that he would continue school. Neituo had failed in the fifth grade so the two were no longer in the same class.

"How big you have grown!" said his grandmother one day.

"Oh, do you really think so, Grandmother?" Mose asked in a pleased voice.

"Yes, see for yourself. You can now reach the top shelf without using a footstool."

"Oh, I have been doing that since last month."

"So like your father when he was your age!"

"He was very tall, wasn't he?"

"No, he was not tall. Our clansmen tend to be stocky and so was your father."

"I always think of him as a tall man."

"Ah, that is because you were too young to remember. Just two years and some months."

Mose was now thirteen and his calves and arms were becoming muscular. He could chop big pieces of wood without any effort. He liked to chop wood for both households, stacking them up separately. It made him feel strong and useful.

"What a blessing you are to us!" Khrienuo said as she helped him stack wood.

"You and Mother have taken care of me long enough. It is time I started to take care of you," he said teasingly.

"Yes, and in another year or two we will find you a wife," she teased back.

"Huh! What do I need a wife for?! I already have two women to look after. I don't need a third!"

Later, when they were seated by the fire, the mood was less jovial. Vilaü had been in the fields all day.

"I came back early because there were a lot of army trucks parked above us on the road. They were there for a long time," she explained. "We were afraid of the soldiers. They simply stood on the road and stared at us as we went past them."

"They keep coming and coming," said Khrienuo. "Early in the morning, I hear army trucks crawling up the road. One must be very cautious when there are so many soldiers about. During the war, a friend of ours was taken away by the Japanese. We didn't ask her what happened but she kept on crying after she came back."

"At school, they have been warning the boys not to wander around after six," said Mose.

"And the boys should heed that warning," said Vilaü, "I have never seen so many soldiers before. There are almost as many soldiers now as we had during the Japanese war."

"It is because our men are asking for independence," Mose explained.

"What will they do to us? They can't force us to become Indian," said Khrienuo.

Mose was silent. For the first time in his life, he felt fearful of the future.

In December, the village was assembled together. A man carefully explained that they were collecting signatures and thumbprints of those who wanted a free Nagaland. They would send all the signatures to the Prime Minister of India and then he would give them their freedom. Mose, Khrienuo and Vilaü readily joined in. There were long lines of people on the appointed day. Several men sat at tables and wrote down the names of the people. When it was Khrienuo's turn, the man showed her how to dip her thumb in ink and press down hard on the paper next to where he had written her name. Vilaü did the same. Mose and Neituo could not vote because they were both underage. The signing took the whole day. Even at the end of the day, there were still people who had not made it to the head of the queue. So, lanterns were lit and the rest of the signatures taken late into the night.

Khrienuo and Vilaü were very pleased they had participated in the plebiscite. Back at home, they reluctantly washed the ink stains off. They were told the next day that the signatures had been collected by men in every village of Nagaland and were being taken to the Prime Minister of India.

"Something should happen now. He can't ignore it when so many villagers have expressed their wishes," Khrienuo spoke confidently.

But nothing happened. In fact, things went from bad to worse. Curfews became the order of the day. Four young men from the Tsutuonuomia clan were arrested for breaking curfew. They were jailed for a week. The new security forces were rough and spoke Hindi. They were armed and carried weapons. Word spread that they had beaten up the arrested men. When released, the men had ugly black and blue bruises.

THE DARKNESS
DESCENDS

Neituo had made some new friends. A group of four boys in his class who excitedly told him all they know about the Naga freedom movement. From them he learned that the Naga leaders had organised the Naga National Council, and were fighting for freedom from India in a peaceful way. The Indian army had now moved into the interior areas of Nagaland and killed a number of villagers. The Naga National Council had sent several letters to the Prime Minister of India. There was talk that they would even write to the United Nations if the killings did not stop.

"There is a protest march on the 18th October," he said to Mose. "Let's go and see."

"But it's not a holiday," Mose protested.

"No, but we'll slip back to school afterwards."

The day of the march, some people carried posters and others marched quietly on. It was a very big group as people had come in from the neighbouring villages. Mose and Neituo came across people from Jotsoma village and Khonoma village that they recognised from their dialect. The men wore their black body-cloths and walked in a straight line along the main road. Their destination was the Deputy Commissioner's office where they would submit a memorandum. The women were in the rear. Mose and Neituo followed the march without actually joining it.

The first marchers were close to the Deputy Commissioner's office when they heard gunshots and loud cries. The boys could not see what was happening but they heard a cry go up, "Someone has been shot!" Paralyzed with fear, they stopped where they were. The marchers scattered in fear. One of the leaders could be heard shouting, "Watch out, a man has been shot!"

The police fired more bullets into the air, which effectively scared off those in the rear. The marchers were scattered, their leaders shoved aside and the man who had been shot dead was taken away. Mose and Neituo were too frightened to stay. They ran homeward, following the throng of marchers who were rushing off in untidy groups.

"My God, what will I tell Mother?" Mose gasped. The two had paused to catch their breaths on the steep path to the village.

"Will she be angry if she finds out where you were?"

"Of course. Especially if she hears that people got shot!"

"I never expected that, never thought they would actually shoot," said Neituo, tears glistening in his eyes.

"Nor I," Mose responded.

"Those policemen. Some of them were laughing as the people went past them," Neituo recalled.

"They must've have known that would happen. How horrible!" said Mose.

Ahead of them, one man was saying angrily,

"We can't let it go. This is too much. We are not *tefü thevo*. We are not animals that they can shoot us when they will. It was a peaceful march." Another man shouted back,

"You are right. They have no reason to shoot us without cause. But we can't fight guns with our bare hands."

News of the shooting in town had travelled very swiftly to the village. Many had heard the gunshots. Vilaü was very anxious for her son. She ran out of her house without her body-cloth. She found him near the Mission Compound.

"*Ayalie*! Never do that again, son!" she scolded. Mose winced a little at her rebuke in public, yet he knew how worried she must have been for him. They went home in silence.

"We didn't think they would shoot, Mother. Neituo and I were not really in the procession. We were walking along and watching," said Mose when they were home.

"These are dangerous times, son. What if something had happened to you? How could I bear it?"

"I won't do it again, Mother."

Khrienuo kept silent. She was wise enough to know that one adult's admonition was sufficient.

"You are precious to us. You are our egg, Mose," was the only sentence he heard from his grandmother.

The next day Mose and Neituo learned that the man who had been shot was from Jotsoma. His name was Zasibito Nagi. The headmaster announced at assembly that curfew had been imposed in town. The teachers in turn, explained this very carefully in class. The new law said that if people were seen

Tefü thevo: dogs and pigs, native term for animals
Ayalie: expression of anxiety, joy or surprise depending on the context

moving around in a group of more than three, they would be arrested immediately. The students understood now that the situation had become very serious. No longer was this just exciting skirmishes with the law that the boys discussed in secretive whispers. It had become something much bigger and it was rapidly spiralling out of control.

ELECTIONS (1952)

After the disastrous peace march, the government came down hard on the people. Curfews were frequently imposed. There was a rumour that the school might be closed down.

"Surely they won't do that, will they?" Mose asked.

"Well, Father says they did that during the Japanese war. Might happen again. I won't be too upset if that happens," Neituo answered.

"But we could lose a year. Don't you see we would be the losers?" Mose went on.

"Not everyone is as fond of studying as you are Mose," Neituo scoffed.

"All right, let's look at it another way. Schools are closed down only in wartime. It's horrible to think we could be in the middle of another war."

"Maybe it won't come to that," said Neituo without managing to sound hopeful.

But the men were not too sure about that. They had their own reasons. Word had got out about the last meeting of the village council. One of the men had spoken harshly about the Prime Minister of India.

"That man Nehru," the man had shouted, "Do you know what Nehru said when he got his copy of the Naga plebiscite? He shook his fist and shouted, 'Whether heaven falls or India goes to pieces and blood runs red in the country, I don't care. Nagas will not be allowed to become independent.' How can we live under such a man? Can we live under such a government?"

The meeting broke up with many expressing anger at the Indian leader.

Neither Mose nor Neituo were old enough to sit in the Village Council meetings. But on Saturdays, they joined other youngsters their age who sat outside the council hall and tried to eavesdrop. Now and again, an elder would come out and shoo them away, "Children, be off with you! This is not for your ears!" The youngsters would run off at this and watch from a distance for the man to go back into the hall. Then they would creep back to listen. The men's voices could be heard quite clearly through the thin walls of the council hall. Never before had the proceedings of the council aroused so much curiosity among the young. They caught snatches of words several times, words like freedom and non-violence and India.

Back at home, Mose listened to the radio for more news, but the only news about India was the preparation for the General Elections.

"Anything new on the radio?" his mother asked.

"Nothing, Mother," Mose answered.

"Oh, all right," she said and went back to her work.

The three of them still conducted their evening ritual with the radio. Nowadays, Mose habitually listened to it in the morning before school.

That evening, he explained to his grandmother and mother what the elections were about. That people would put their thumbprints or signatures on little pieces of paper to vote for the person they wanted for Prime Minister of India. "Oh, that's exactly what we did last year. We gave our thumb prints to vote for independence," said Khrienuo.

"Yes, it is something similar," said Mose.

"Well, we don't have to vote for the Prime Minister of India. That's none of our business," Khrienuo stated very firmly.

"You are right, Grandmother, it's none of our business who gets elected Prime Minister of India."

Later, there was nothing on the radio about the empty ballot boxes that were returned from Nagaland. People got to know about it from the few Nagas working in the Government sector. It was retold in whispers.

The next election was not so uneventful. It was scheduled to be held on a working day. Mose and Neituo were on their way to school when they were rudely stopped by a policeman.

"How old are you?" asked the policeman roughly as he pointed a gun in Mose's face.

"Fi...fi..fifteen," he stammered in reply.

"Are you sure?"

"Yes, yes sir," Mose replied.

The policeman thrust him aside and asked Neituo the same question.

They were both in their school uniforms and there was little doubt that they were too young to vote.

"What shall we do?" they whispered to each other.

"Let's go on to school," Mose replied, "should be safer there."

But when they reached the school yard, it was closed and

a big notice was hung on the main door: SCHOOL CLOSED DUE TO ELECTION.

That was all. The two friends slowly made their way back. They took the short cut through the Tsütuonuomia clan areas, hoping to avoid the rough policeman. There was no one at home when they reached. After an hour, Vilaü and Khrienuo came home together.

"Mother," called out Mose.

The two women entered the house, grey-faced. They did not smile. Vilaü's hair was in an untidy knot.

"What's the matter? Where have you been?" Mose asked.

They didn't reply immediately. Entering the house, Khrienuo sat down heavily.

"Shall I get you a glass of water?" Vilaü asked solicitously.

"Thank you," said Khrienuo.

"What happened?" Mose asked them again.

"After you left for school, we were at home, getting the mats out to dry paddy when we heard some shouting. So we stopped our work and went to see. Suddenly there were policemen and soldiers all over the village. They pointed guns at people and assembled them all at the Village council. Everyone we knew was there. And there were people from the other clans that we didn't know.

The policeman forced us to put our thumbprints on little pieces of paper and put it in a box. There were several boxes. A man refused to do as they said. One of the policemen hit him on the side of his head with his rifle and he fell to the ground. After that, everyone did as they were told and put their thumbprints on the papers.

We didn't want to do it. We could see none of the others

wanted to do it either. But there was no way we could avoid it. They knew our names and our husbands' names...."

Vilaü's voice broke as she came to the last sentence.

"Hush Mother, you don't have to tell me anymore. I understand what happened now. Neituo and I were stopped by a policeman too but we showed him our bags and told him we were school children."

"Oh! it is wrong," said Khrienuo, "what they are doing is so wrong..."

OCCUPATION

"Have you ever seen so many soldiers before?" Mose asked Neituo.

"Never. My father says that even during the Japanese war, they had only half the number of soldiers than what we have here now."

The two were watching convoys of army vehicles climbing up the Dimapur-Kohima road.

"It's terrible. You hear the convoys every night, don't you?"

"Father says that we don't know even a fraction of what the people in the interior are going through," said Neituo grimly.

"Curfews? Village groupings? I have heard a few stories," said Mose.

"Worse, much worse. News keeps trickling in everyday. The Indian army has burnt several Ao and Sema villages and raped women and killed some gaonburas. In some villages, they have killed many innocent people."

"Why?" Mose asked.

"They said these were people helping the Undergrounds,"

Neituo replied, using the name by which the Naga army was now commonly called.

"How do they know?" Mose asked.

"They don't know. They kill a few to put fear in the rest to prevent them from helping the Undergrounds."

They were both frightened at the events that had suddenly overtaken the quiet lives of the villagers. After the forced election, the police and the army closed in everywhere. The villagers saw them hiding in the woods when they went to the fields.

"Women, be very careful," the elders warned.

No one dared venture out on curfew nights. Even the drunks stayed home and drank in the safety of their own houses.

School was very unstable, closing frequently for days at a time. Sporadic shooting broke out in town one evening. It shocked everyone and people went scurrying home. Soon after that more and more young men disappeared. Men in their twenties, unmarried young men. Some were educated, some not, the uneducated ones outnumbered the others.

"Beilie's son has joined the Underground," Khrienuo said flatly when Mose and Vilaü were with her.

"When did you hear of it?" Vilaü asked.

"This afternoon. Beilie's wife is inconsolable, she was weeping as though her son had died.'"

"That whole age-group has gone then," remarked Vilaü.

"More than half," said Mose. "The married ones are still around."

The age-group they were talking about was two groups above Mose's. Vilaü's heart constricted at the thought of that. Would this new war go on so long as to take her son off too? She did not want to think about that.

There was a growing public anger at the atrocities being committed on Naga civilians by the Indian army. Three members of the Naga National Council had been killed and their bodies displayed publicly in town. People were forced to watch as the soldiers stood guard and mocked the dead men. Everyone was shocked. It created the fear that the army hoped it would. At the same time, it roused deep anger in the community.

"Doesn't our culture teach us that when a relative is murdered we should avenge his death? I do not want to fail in my cultural duty," said Viguolie, the younger brother of one of the murdered men. Soon after he left to join the Underground. These men took whatever weapons they could find with them. Old shotguns, rusty Japanese guns that had evaded the gun collection by the British government after the war, or just crude daos.

They left at night and their departure was spoken of in whispers amongst their fellow villagers. Around the same time shadowy figures were seen in the village. Young men were being recruited into the Underground. They came and went without a trace.

In the safety of their home Khrienuo, Vilaü and Mose put the radio on to see if there would be any mention of these strange happenings in their land. Nothing. "Don't they say anything of the men killed last week?" Khrienuo asked.

"No," said Mose.

"Listen again, Mose, maybe they will talk about it," his grandmother insisted. But there was never any mention of the horrors at home on the radio.

The next day was a fire-genna day. It was taboo to make fire in the fields. Khrienuo and Vilaü prepared to go to the fields late with cooked food. Though they had been Christians for six years now, they still observed the taboo days of the non-Christians. It was pointless to get into an argument with the few who still followed the old religion and dictated the taboos.

"Don't work too hard," Mose called out, as he was leaving for school. "I'll come to help you after school."

"Thank you, son."

Soon, the two women left for the field. They were joined by one of their neighbours, Neituo's mother, Kezevinuo.

"My husband says we should come home early. Soldiers have been seen loitering in the woods near our fields," said the neighbour.

"*Hou*, Aviü, that is not a good thing at all, we must heed what your husband says," Vilaü replied.

"Yes, we mustn't stay late though it is tempting to keep working and try to finish as much as possible," Khrienuo added.

"They say many women in the Sema areas have been raped," Kezevinuo continued.

"Oh, poor souls, who is there to protect us from all these evils?" Khrienuo lamented.

A SHOT IN THE FIELDS

The women did not loiter in the fields when they had finished for the day. There was such a sense of being watched that they hurriedly finished their work and prepared to go home. Vilaü cleaned her hoe and placed it in her basket.

"Mother, I'm going to wash my hands and feet and get ready," she called to Khrienuo.

"Go ahead, I will join you soon," Khrienuo answered.

Vilaü was washing her hands by the stream when she heard gunshots ring out. Had her ears deceived her? Or were those really gunshots?

"Mother.." She called out to Khrienuo. There was no response. Vilaü turned around.

At the edge of the field, someone was lying in a dark heap.

"Nooo!" Vilaü screamed as she ran towards her mother-in-law.

The bullet that had entered the back of her head had killed her. Vilaü's cries brought people running from the neighbouring fields. They tried to revive Khrienuo but it was too late. So they quickly rigged up a stretcher with a body-cloth and two branches and the men took turns to carry her home. Vilaü followed the small group of people, weeping loudly. That was the sight that met Mose's eyes when he was coming to meet his mother and grandmother. There was no sign of his grandmother. On the other hand, his mother looked like a frenzied wretch, beating her chest and throwing her body-cloth away when she caught sight of him.

"Mother! What's wrong?" he called out as he ran toward the group. They stopped when he approached them. Running up to them, he saw it was his grandmother on the stretcher. With a cry he took her hand. It was still warm to his touch but she had been dead an hour. Mose watched in disbelief. Then he cried and cried like a child. After some time a deep rage overpowered his sorrow, and he had no more tears left. The group carrying the stretcher slowed down as they tried to tell the boy about the shooting.

"Soldiers. We have seen them for the past five days in our woods," said one of the men. "We thought that if they saw us peacefully cultivating our fields, they would not harm us. But when we finished working, there was a shout and they began to shoot towards the fields. We don't know if they were trying to scare us or if they were aiming at us and missing. It happened so fast. One of the shots hit your grandmother. I'm sorry lad, this is such a terrible thing."

Mose and his mother had no male relatives except Beilie. Their clansmen came and arranged Khrienuo's funeral. There was loud weeping all night. In the middle of the night, there was a heated argument amongst some of the men who were keeping vigil.

"We cannot allow this to happen again," said a young man.

"What can we do? Run after them with daos and spears?"

Three of the men who were present began to talk about it loudly.

An old man came out of the house and said,

"Have you no respect for the dead? It is taboo to raise your voice near the deceased."

That quietened them immediately and they carried on their debate in lowered voices.

"No one is happy," said the second man. "But we must be well-armed, if we are to do anything."

"And proceed with good planning, not rush into it."

The next morning the pastor came and conducted the funeral solemnly. There were many women present. Beilie spoke at the funeral: "I am speaking on behalf of the family today, not because I have contributed to looking after them, but I am speaking because I am the only male relative. My aunt has always been a very hardworking and self-respecting woman. She worked hard to feed her only son when she was a young widow. She never wanted to be a burden to the family or the clan. When her son died, our sister-in-law Vilaü became a daughter to her, and they have looked after each other all these years. Together they have brought up her grandson, Mose, to be a fine young member of the clan. I want to thank all of you for attending her funeral. The circumstances of my aunt's death are very unfortunate. We have lost a very fine mother and grandmother today. Our family is bereaved. Our clan is sharing in that bereavement. I thank you all for the honour you have shown us in coming to share in our grief."

Distant relatives and some of their clansmen kept Mose and Vilaü company for a week after Khrienuo's funeral.

They didn't know that the shooting had been documented in the army files and the soldier in question would not face prosecution. He was protected by the Assam Maintenance of Public Order Act 1953. The Act empowered a soldier to "shoot and kill, in case it is felt necessary to do so for maintaining of public order."

Mose's cold grief worried the others greatly. The young man, for he was 17 now, had sat stony-faced throughout the funeral. They knew how close he had been to his grandmother. On the third evening, Mose was sitting by the fire. One of their relatives lifted the radio down and asked if Mose could turn it on. Mose fiddled with the knobs and suddenly, a teardrop fell on the radio. With great heaving sobs, Mose mourned his grandmother who had loved this radio and eagerly listened to it every evening. He could recall that first day when they had bought it and listened to it every night so enthusiastically. Grandmother would impatiently finish her evening meal so they could listen to the radio. He sobbed for a long time and they let him. Vilaü placed her arm round him and waited it out.

"There is a time for everything," said Neituo's mother. "Do not staunch weeping when it is the time for weeping."

"I'm all right now, Aunt," Mose replied, controlling his sobbing.

"It is nothing to be ashamed of my child. All of us are mourning her."

"I am not ashamed to mourn my grandmother. She was the kindest woman I knew."

MOVING ON

The two of them were completely shattered by the sudden death of Khrienuo. Vilaü did not do any field-work for almost a month. They moped around the house, or wandered about her house aimlessly. For a few days after the funeral, Vilaü found things to do in her mother-in-law's house. She went through Khrienuo's personal belongings and decided what to do with her things. Her mother-in-law had always had neat habits. In a trunk were her old body-cloths, and waist-cloths belonging to her mother. Vilaü put them aside to be sorted through another day. They had buried her with some of the cloths.

Vilaü found a bag that held papers and some files. Khrienuo had had a lot of respect for paper. Perhaps because she had been illiterate. She would carefully fold what she considered as important papers and keep them away in a bag. These Vilaü kept aside so that Mose could look through them.

In the kitchen, Khrienuo's store of dried herbs hung in a basket above the hearth. Vilaü took down the basket and laid it near the door, intending to take it to her own house and use whatever was edible. No food was ever wasted. Excess vegetable crops were dried for use in the winter months. Khrienuo, like any other meticulous housekeeper, had done that and stored dried herbs. In another basket, Vilaü found different seeds of vegetables kept aside for the next planting season.

Vilaü kept the fire burning at her mother-in-law's house. Frequently making a fire would keep out the musty smell that abandoned houses acquired if they were not being lived in. People said that such houses felt neglected and slowly fell apart. Vilaü had no intention of letting this happen to her mother-in-law's house. She and Mose would see to it that.

Before she died, Khrienuo had said one day, "When I'm gone, Mose can have my house when he marries. That way they will be close to you, Vilaü. It is a very good thing to have your children close to you. I know because I have had you two and what a joy it has been."

"We won't let you die now, Mother, don't talk of things like that," Vilaü had replied then.

"It is important to talk of such things. If I don't tell you now when I am alive, someday you may be put into a situation where you will wonder, why didn't Mother tell me anything about this?"

Remembering their conversation now, Vilaü recognised the wisdom of the older woman's words. She had been as close to her as her own mother. The elders always took care to tell their children what should be done about their belongings when they were no more, because if they didn't there might be disputes over that. Lands and fields were divided among the heirs. In Khrienuo's case, Mose would inherit all her lands and property as the only male grandson. This was the custom after all. There were no other close relatives who could object to the settlement.

Vilaü swept the mud floor carefully. Then she blew out the lantern by the bed. Remembering to take the papers with her, she locked the door after her and went home. Mose had not come back yet. Vilaü made the fire in her own kitchen and began to make the evening meal.

"Mother!" called out Mose as he entered the door, "Sorry I'm late."

"Don't be out late when there is curfew, son," said Vilaü.

"There's nothing on this evening, Mother. I was talking to friends in town," he explained.

"You know I worry if you come back late."

"I am careful Mother, you should know that."

After dinner, she brought him the papers she had found in Khrienuo's house.

"You should take a look at these and decide what to do with them," she said. Mose moved his chair closer to the lantern and tried to read.

"Where did you find these, Mother?"

"At your grandmother's."

Mose went through them by the light of the lantern.

"Very interesting. Did Grandfather go to school? Did he know how to read?"

"He worked for the British government. He did a lot of coolie work, but I don't think he went to school."

Mose lifted a paper to the light and read out,

"This letter is dated 1929...oh, it is the Simon Commission, of course!" exclaimed Mose. "Mother, our people have been asking to be independent from 1929, imagine that!" Mose spoke excitedly. He read the letter and then told his mother, "This was signed by twenty men, Mother. What an excellent letter. Such clear reasons for Nagas to be separate from India and Burma. If only they had taken heed of that in their time."

"I don't understand what all that is about, son. You will have to decide if the paper is to be thrown away or kept safely somewhere."

"Let me look at the other papers, Mother."

"They are all in that bag."

Mose rummaged through the papers. They were some Government papers about the land his grandfather had been gifted in Dimapur.

"I will keep the papers, Mother, but not in our house. I think it's safer to keep it in Grandmother's house. The army has begun to conduct searches of houses. Neituo told me that a man from Khonoma village was arrested because they found a copy of this very letter in his house. He was beaten badly too."

"Oh son, should we keep the papers at all then?"

"If it's not in our house, I think it will be all right. I will hide it carefully in Grandmother's house."

"All right son."

MOSE LEAVES SCHOOL

1956. At 19, Mose felt his mother was passing on to him the reins of their household. Vilaü was forty-one but she looked much older. She had gotten more grey in her hair after her mother-in-law's death.

Mose had not finished school in 1954. His grandmother had been killed at the end of his school year. He didn't have the heart to study for his final exams.

The next year he had gone to school with the junior class. Neituo was also with the junior class as he had failed in the ninth grade. They were as tall as their teachers now. Their classmates were a year or two younger than them.

"You must try and complete your tenth this year," said the Headmaster. He looked directly at Neituo and Mose when he said this. "We are not sure if school can continue next year. We have had warnings that it may be closed down."

He didn't need to stress that this was because of the growing unrest. Some students had been taken out of school by their parents and sent to study in Shillong. These were the children from rich families. The others who couldn't afford to do that stayed on.

One afternoon, just as school was closing for the day, shooting broke out. There was pandemonium in town. That same afternoon, a wedding was scheduled to be held. Guests who were buying gifts at the Doss and Co stores, dropped whatever they had chosen, and ran homeward. The town reverberated with the exchange of fire. People ran helter skelter trying to avoid the bullets which seemed to be coming from all directions.

Mose and Neituo were on their way home when they saw four men being beaten by the army. The men covered their bleeding heads with their hands but the soldiers continued to rain down blows at them. One man lay unconscious on the ground, but the soldiers did not stop kicking him in the head. The two boys ran off as one of the soldiers shouted out in Hindi, "Hey you two! Stop!" The boys quickly ran into an alley and, once out of reach of the soldiers, scurried home. The two of them knew there was nothing they could do to help the men who were being attacked by the soldiers. For both, it was horrifying to see and they were still trembling when they neared their houses. They had heard stories of people being killed and tortured in the villages but not until today had they seen the brutality of the army attacks.

"My God, those poor men. Do you think the one on the ground is dead?" Mose asked. They were both short of breath.

"Most likely. Even if he recovers, he will surely suffer brain damage," Neituo replied, panting as he finished.

"I didn't think they would do that in broad daylight. No place is safe now," said Mose.

"No. It's terrible," said Neituo in a trembling voice. "I hated running away but if we had stayed, they would have beaten us too."

"Those men! They were not armed, they were just innocent civilians," said Mose in a horrified tone.

"It's the only way they can get at the others, by torturing innocents and turning them against those who have gone underground," answered Neituo.

"Do you think that is what they're trying to do?" Mose asked anxiously.

"Well, there are already some people who are opposed to the conflict and they blame the fighting on the Undergrounds," said Neituo.

"Who are they? No one could want Nagaland to become part of India. Those who are against our freedom struggle must be opportunists. Everyone I know wants to be independent, even illiterate villagers. If Mother would be all right on her own, I'd join the movement right away."

The two parted after some time, knowing that if they were late, their parents would be worried. Mose's mother was standing at the doorway looking out for him.

"Son, were you anywhere near the shooting?" she asked.

"No Mother, we were halfway home when it happened."

"Oh, son what is our life coming to?"

Mose decided not to tell her about the men they had seen being beaten.

"Mother, I don't want to continue with school anymore."

"Why son? You're almost ready to finish."

"I don't feel right to be studying when we are living in such troubled times. Let me take over the field-work so you can stay at home safely."

"What makes you think I'd be safer at home, son? They are everywhere, and they attack everyone. Only Jisu keeps us safe."

"Do you really think so, Mother?"

"Oh son, why else have we escaped harm? We have to keep trusting in Jisu."

Mose did not have his mother's faith. So much was happening that was incomprehensible. He knew there were many more people being killed than the numbers that reached them. He joined a group of men who sent letters to the Indian Prime Minister about the killings. They also wrote several letters to the United Nations. Mose learned that the leaders of the Naga National Council had written to the British House of Lords even before Indian independence. What was there left to do? The leaders seemed to have done everything that they could possibly do.

Regarding the shooting in town, the army claimed to have been fired on and therefore they had shot into civilian quarters. Of the four men who were beaten three died on the spot, and the fourth died in hospital. The army claimed they were members of the Underground. But the truth was, none of them were linked to the Underground in any way. Besides the four men, a woman and her two daughters had also been shot dead in the firing.

MOSE AND NEITUO JOIN UP

After the shooting, the school was closed by an order issued by the District Commissioner. It stated that it was too dangerous for children to be walking to and from school in such an environment.

A few days after the shooting in town, a woman of Kohima village went missing. Mose and Neituo joined the men who went to search for her. They carried their daos and went out in a group of thirty. Mose and Neituo were scouring the long grass when they saw something lying on a rock. The two gagged when they realised what it was. A limb.

The missing woman had been raped and murdered and decapitated. There was great anger at her funeral. Men spoke loudly of revenge and no one quieted them because this had never happened before. The soldiers who had done it made no secret of their crime.

"We will do that to all those who oppose us," sneered the Captain.

That night, Mose spent a long time explaining to his

mother why he was joining the Naga Underground. In the end she simply said,

"Do what you have to do, son, and may Jisu go with you."

"Mother, you do understand that I have to help our people, don't you? I am going so this will not happen again."

"I will try and understand, son. I don't yet, but I will try."

Vilaü remembered what the midwife had said at Mose's birth. "This one is going to be a warrior one day," she had announced. Vilaü knew that a woman could not stand between a man and his destiny, even if the man was her son.

She didn't want him to feel bad about leaving her. So she said she would be all right, with Kezevinuo for company. Mose did not tell her that Neituo would leave without telling his parents. Neituo's parents were very opposed to the idea of him joining up. So he had decided to simply leave in the night without telling them.

Two days later, the boys were gone! In a group with twenty others. They were not told their destination. So their family did not know their whereabouts at all. The Undergrounds did that to protect both the family and the new members. The army had begun to identify and harass the relatives of those in the Underground in an effort to make the members surrender.

Neituo's mother was weeping loudly when she discovered her son gone. The news spread quickly to the rest of the clan. In a way, however, Neituo's silent departure saved the families because the report which reached the Indian army was that two boys had left without telling their parents. This way, the army would have no grounds to interrogate the family members.

Vilaü was just as disconsolate as Kezevinuo. She decided not to tell them that Mose had taken her permission to go.

"He used to speak about it but I didn't think he had any intention of joining up," she said to clanspeople who enquired about her son.

Tears came easily to her as she was missing her son dearly.

"Pray God will protect him," said the women who came to see her.

They themselves hoped such a fate would not befall them.

The incident did not pass quietly. If anything, it made the army more vigilant than ever. They went to each house in the village to do a head count. In a register of names, the *gaonburas* were ordered to list the names of all the members of the household. If any male members were in the Underground, they were to make a separate list of those families. The villagers fearfully submitted their names. No one thought of lying about members in the Underground. Mose's clan had about twenty men in the organization already. The other clans ranged between thirty and forty men. The head count alarmed the army to the increasing ranks of the Underground. It also made the villagers realize how many of their men had now joined up. These were things that had been spoken of in whispers, now they were out in the open.

Some of the boys made very furtive visits under cover of darkness to meet their families and collect rations. On such visits, they came by night speaking in whispers. As the conflict grew, with no signs of a solution in sight, it became more and more dangerous to be associated with the Undergrounds.

"Will they not come on a visit?" Vilaü whispered to Kezevinuo. How sorely they missed their sons! They had not had news of them except for a message from an older Underground member. "The young ones are well but we cannot tell you where they are, let that be enough for now," was the message relayed to them through another person.

It was very strange and unfamiliar but they learned to get used to the ways of the Underground. Members were not spoken of in public. Some adopted nicknames by which they were known amongst a trusted circle of friends. Vilaü felt great anxiety for her son when she thought of all that was said about warriors in the village.

"Warriors cannot have progeny," was what people often said of them.

"Warriors have a shorter life-span than other men," she had heard that too.

Yet, not everything that was said of warriors was negative:

"If it is not their time, the sharpest spear will not touch them," her mother used to say that.

"Oh Jisu," she cried aloud and then half-sighed, half-whispered into the darkness, "Oh Jisu, you have to protect them!"

THE JUNGLE YEARS

Mose and Neituo were not the youngest in the group. There were two other boys aged barely seventeen. They were from the Chakhesang tribe and their parents had been killed by the Indian army. Very young boys. They were intent on finishing the training at the top of the list. Both Mose and Neituo were very surprised to see girls amongst the cadres. Months of training had built up their muscles and they deftly handled guns, something that Mose and Neituo were yet to learn. There was in particular a tall girl who spoke roughly to them. Her name was Neilhounuo and Mose vaguely remembered that she had been to school with them, a year or two junior to them. He couldn't recollect if she had passed sixth grade. Probably not. She looked as though she had spent years in the jungles.

The camp was two days' walk from Kohima. It lay close to the Northern Angami forests. Cleverly camouflaged sheds had been built of bamboo and leaves. Piles of leaves on the floor of the sheds made up sleeping quarters for the soldiers. When they lay down to sleep, Mose inhaled the strong smell of soil rising up from below them.

"This is what we wanted to do, right?" Neituo asked in the night.

"Yes, of course, we are doing the right thing," was Mose's reply.

"No regrets?"

"None."

"Can you bear to get up in the morning then?" Neituo asked.

"Must we discuss that now?" Mose replied with a grimace.

The next day Neituo cut his hand on a sharp piece of bamboo while making a shelter. Mose quickly plucked some bitter wormwood and made a paste of it. He laid it on the wound and it immediately stopped the blood flow. He then took a bit of the leaf and stuck it behind Neituo's ear.

"What's that for? My hand's bleeding, not my ear!" Neituo exclaimed.

"It keeps the bad spirits away. The ones that make you do crazy things," Mose responded.

"Well, it will certainly keep the girls away. Yeesh! What a smell!"

Life in the Underground was rigorous. They had been warned about that, but they were eager to take it all in. Everyone woke in the early hours, way before dawn. Exercises and training began after tea. After two weeks, they shifted camp. That soon became routine for them. The trainees felt exhausted from the unaccustomed harshness of their new lifestyle. Their overworked muscles protested when they lay down in their rough sleeping bags. It took months for them to get used to the pounding their bodies received.

After the period of physical training, they learned to use rifles, running with them and stopping to load them quickly.

They never shot a bullet. One, because the sound would reveal their whereabouts, and two, because they had very limited supplies of ammunitions. Food was meagre too, and though they developed the stringy muscles of hunters, they lost much weight in the first months.

The older ones liked the two newcomers. Mose's respectful nature endeared him to his superior officers and peers alike, and Neituo's sense of humour won him many friends. In the afternoons they willingly foraged for food. One afternoon, together with two others, they approached some women working in a field and asked for food. The women readily gave them what they had, but reprimanded them as their mothers would. "*Hou* my sons! You should not come out in the open so boldly. The jungle has eyes and ears everywhere now! Go back quickly and come out only at night and even then, as stealthily as moles." Smiling sheepishly they retreated into the woods with their gifts of food.

They moved camp a second time. Very quietly by night. Mose and Neituo were a little unsure of their exact location. They had moved out of the Northern Angami forest areas and shifted closer to the Chakhesang territories where the forests were much more dense. Trainees were not told of their location for fear that, if captured, they could be tortured into revealing the location of the camp. Furthermore, Mose and Neituo had not travelled much beyond Kohima town and the nearby villages. Certainly not to the Chakhesang areas. So they had no idea where they were. Villages in the distance looked very much the same to them.

After three months in the woods, Neituo felt very homesick. Mose found him with his head in his hands. He had not come to eat the evening meal.

"Are you sick?" he asked.

"I am so homesick, I don't know if I can continue any longer."

Mose looked closely at his friend. Neituo was crying unashamedly.

"I miss my family so much and I know my mother will be very worried because I never told her," he blurted out.

"They're not likely to let us go back so easily," Mose stated. "In any case, the army will be looking for us. We can't just reappear in the village. We'll be picked up, questioned, beaten, the truth tortured out of us. Have you forgotten the four men we saw on the day of the firing?"

"I know all that. I just wish I had had the courage to tell my mother I was leaving. If I had been man enough then, I wouldn't feel so bad now."

It was a difficult situation. Mose did not feel mature enough to offer his friend advice on it. Perhaps they could send a message, or perhaps they could even sneak back home and meet their parents.

They asked one of their batchmates about it, but the idea of sneaking back was vetoed by him.

"It's too dangerous to sneak back," he said. "In fact, if you tried that, you could be courtmartialled on your return."

"Why? We would surely return, it wouldn't be as though we were leaving," Mose said.

"You know there is a reason why they ask you several times if you are committed to the cause. They don't just take you after your first promise. They want to see you are committed enough."

"A letter then?" Mose suggested.

"Maybe a message by word of mouth. We could leave that

at the next village, and it is less dangerous for the ones who will carry the message."

So they devised a message to be sent to their parents to say that they were safe. Beyond that, they couldn't say more. The message network was effective. In a few weeks they heard back from the messenger that their families were well too, and praying for them.

Neituo felt much better having sent the message. His mother sent her own special message. It was worded carefully but he understood it at once. It meant that she was no longer angry at him. It soothed his young mind.

The two of them focused on their trainings more intensely. They sincerely believed that if they did their best as soldiers of the Underground Naga army, their land would be freed soon. Their leaders told them that as many as ten thousand men, women and children had now been killed by the Indian army.

THE FLAG

When it was two weeks to August 15, the Indian Independence day, the Underground began to plan to hoist the Naga flag at the Kohima stadium. Mose volunteered to climb the silk-cotton tree in the centre of the stadium and hoist the flag. It would be extremely dangerous as the town was under curfew. Any movement was risky. A Naga doctor had been shot dead when the army saw him wander out into his front yard during curfew hours.

Mose was aware of the great risks involved in the mission. Excitedly, he prepared for the trip. Mose was well liked by his senior officer. He was smart and always eager to learn more. They believed he could do the job as he was an expert tree climber. Further, he was cool-headed in spite of his youth. Mose and two others left for Kohima on the 13th of August under cover of night. Always keeping to the shortcuts and field paths, they finally reached the Chotobosti area and rested there.

After that they used a side path to get to the town. When they reached the stadium, Mose's hands were trembling. Army patrols were out and about in the streets. He crawled to

the stadium alone, carrying the flag in a small backpack. His
two friends were waiting near the old school building, pistols
drawn. But they would not come further. Mose crawled
forward, inch by inch towards the unguarded stadium. The
distance seemed unending.

Sweating profusely, he neared the tree, he paused a bit and
then raised his head to listen for sounds. It was so still he
could hear the night insects. Slowly he got up on his knees
and hands. Not a soul was around. He climbed the tree and
carefully began to fasten the flag onto the tree. At first he
was so nervous that he nearly dropped the flag. Steadying
himself, he managed to tie the makeshift pole to the tree.
The unfurled flag rose above the tree and moved in the wind.
In the morning, the wind would lift it high for all to see.
As silently as he had come, Mose climbed down and made
his way out of the stadium. He joined his friends, and they
disappeared into the night like shadows.

The next morning the flag flew in the wind for an hour
while whispers went round the village and town, and everyone
came out to see the Naga flag in the stadium. The blue flag
with a rainbow stretched across its breadth and a white star
glowing above, brought tears to the eyes of everyone who
saw it. Some people began to shout, "Long live Nagaland!"
Young boys took it up defiantly and repeated the refrain. A
group of people automatically began to sing, "God bless my
Nagaland." The shouting and the singing alerted the police to
what had happened.

In minutes an army jeep with armed soldiers swung into
the town square. Braking sharply, four soldiers clambered
out and began to shoot at the flag. They didn't go near to
remove it, possibly fearing a trap. Instead they kept shooting

at it for long minutes till it was shot to shreds. The strands of blue cloth hung down grotesquely.

After the incident of the flag-hoisting, the Indian army launched fresh searches for the Undergrounds with even greater intensity. They were sought out in their jungle camps and hideouts and tortured agonizingly to make them confess the names and whereabouts of their comrades when they were caught. The longer they held out, the more unbearable became the torture. Many died and those who survived were maimed for life. Whenever one member of the Naga Underground was caught, the others would break up camp and flee elsewhere to avoid detection and capture. The villagers suffered greatly in these operations. The army had long discovered that terrorizing the villagers could yield some information on the Undergrounds. Village elders were targeted and tortured until they confessed or died from the torture.

Mose's group moved camp twice in three weeks. The village closest to their camp had been burnt. The granaries smouldered for days and the villagers fled to find shelter in the woods. More and more villages were being burnt in this manner. Food supplies ran out for Mose's group. They now knew long days of starvation when they would all share a gourd scavenged from the fields, or a wild animal that they had knifed because they could not risk using their guns.

One afternoon, to Mose's surprise, Neilhounuo shared with him some cocoyam that she had dug up. He gave a bit to Neituo.

"She likes you," Neituo teased. Mose blushed at that but the idea was not repugnant to him.

When they managed to trap and kill a wild animal, they cooked it over smokeless fires, fires that were made under a thick blanket of leaves to prevent the smoke from rising up. An open fire was always avoided because it could give away their whereabouts to the ever alert Indian army.

The army's objective in burning villages and torturing the villagers was to cut off the lifeline for the Underground members effectively. Almost every week reports of rapes and killings poured in. Villages that were grouped together and starved for days had large numbers of deaths.

Mose and Neituo felt angry and helpless when they heard these reports because their officers were not ready to launch counter-attacks. They had seen some of the villagers with horrific wounds on their bodies.

"We should show them that we can fight back too," said Neituo.

"We know who would be made to suffer again then, don't we?" asked Mose.

Counter attacks finally took place when the Undergrounds captured a police outpost near Chiecha village. They took away all the arms and ammunitions they found. The attack came after the terribly brutal torture of villagers by the army. In subsequent attacks on police outposts, the Underground took away more arms. These were distributed among the older trainees.

"It is not our objective to kill the Indian soldiers first," said one of the officers. "Remember that any action on your part must be guided entirely by self-defence. There will come a time for us to attack, but for now we need to stay low and build up our strength. We are not strong enough to fight the Indian army head on, and besides the retaliation against the civilians would be terrible." He lifted up his rifle and spoke again,

"This is the last alternative. We are giving you guns to show India that we mean what we said about staying independent. But when you have a gun in your hands, remember you don't have the right to shoot first."

It was an especially hard lesson for the young men who were deeply angered by what they had seen and heard.

"Why let us join up then?" mumbled a young trainee.

"This is not an ordinary war," shouted the officer, "this is a test of who has the stronger heart. The Indians may have more men and more guns, but this is our ancestral land to which we are bonded. The Indian soldier does not feel for the land as we do. Sooner or later we will defeat them. One day, they will have to retreat and admit that we were right."

VILAÜ

Mose had seen his mother only once in this period. She was thinner and her hair had gone quite gray. She travelled to Rükhroma to meet him at a relative's house. They were overjoyed to see each other. Vilaü held her son to her and clung to his arm as they spoke. It was a very brief meeting because it was dangerous for him to stay more than a few hours.

"Maybe I can come home soon, Mother. They say there will be a cease-fire," he said happily.

"Is that true, son? Will we really see peace in our land?" asked his Mother.

"That is what we were told, Mother. Let's hope it leads to a good solution afterwards."

"Will you come home for good, son? And lead a normal life?"

"I hope so, Mother, I really hope so."

Mose did not tell his mother that many feared the negotiations might be a ruse by the Indian government to close off all the links the Underground had now made with China and Pakistan.

Two trips to Pakistan and one to China had successfully procured them more arms and training. On the first trip to Pakistan, the Nagas were put in prison for some days before the Pakistanis could ascertain their claims. When trust was established, the Pakistani generals gave them excellent training and arms to take back to fight India.

The first trip to China took a great toll on lives. They walked through Burmese territory where the Burmese army was on alert. Some skirmishes took place in which lives were lost. Then came the arduous crossing of the Saramati range, where the extreme weather and roughness of the land claimed even more lives. The ones who reached China were questioned and imprisoned for some days. The Chinese were just as suspicious as the Pakistanis. But when some form of communication had taken place, they gave the Nagas medical care and military training. The teams returned with Chinese made arms to Nagaland.

In the battles with the Indian army, the Underground had first gained the upper hand. Because of this even more troops were poured into Nagaland, and even more villages were burnt.

The increased presence of Indian soldiers meant that the brutal attacks on the villages continued unabated, one of these occurred close to Mose's camp. Six people were tortured and killed on the charge that they had given food to the Undergrounds.

Mose and Neituo joined the others in a carefully planned counter- attack on the army camp that had killed the villagers. It was a pre-dawn attack. They crawled through the undergrowth and positioned themselves above the sleeping camp. The sentry was taken care of by one of the men who sneaked up and knifed the startled jawan before he could shout.

The group then rushed into the camp hurling grenades and shooting into the tents. Frightened shouts filled the air as most of the soldiers in the camp were taken totally by surprise. Mose and Neituo shot at the two officers who were running out of their tents, brandishing their pistols. The first man fell to the ground, but the second continued to come forward firing his pistol. A bullet hit one of the Undergrounds and he fell down dead.

Mose shot at the officer again, a carefully aimed shot that made him topple over. After that they easily took over the camp and seized all the arms and ammunitions they found. The survivors were tied up and left behind. The Undergrounds disappeared into the jungles with their cache of arms.

In the next couple of months they ambushed several Indian army patrols, and took away their guns after killing them. The patrols were easy pickings as they were unfamiliar with both the terrain and the tactics. After a while, Mose's group stopped the ambushes, worried that they were becoming too predictable. By then they had gathered over 50 rifles, but ammunition was still in short supply. Nevertheless, they withdrew to the new camp deep in the jungle for a well deserved rest.

When two months had passed, they received some disquieting news.

"Spies," said Neituo.

"Are you sure?" asked Mose incredulously, "How could that be?"

"I know that there are some who are doing it for the money," said Neituo, "and others because of clan rivalry."

They were talking about two men who had been captured and brought to their camp. They were being interrogated by the officers because they were thought to be behind the capture and killing of a General in the Underground. Only three people, including one of the two men, had known the General was to be at a certain village on a particular day.

On the third day the spies were led out of the camp, handcuffed. Everyone knew they would be executed. They also knew the spies were better off dying at the hands of their own men than going back to face the Indian army. Mose shuddered at the thought. It was one thing to be shooting at an enemy soldier. But to have to shoot at someone from your own village or clan, that was almost murder even if the man were a traitor. He looked at Neituo and knew he felt the same.

"If you let them go and they return to the Indian army, they will be tortured and killed. That's what the Indian army does to spies that have been exposed by the Naga army. Nobody likes to execute one of his own people but treachery has to be stamped out with the harshest punishment," their officer explained.

"They don't really deserve to live, but how I wish it wouldn't be us who have to mete out judgement," Neituo said to Mose in a low voice.

After the executions they had to move camp again, this time further eastward. It was a two-day walk to find the new camp site and establish that there were no Indian army outposts close by. They were quite close to the Indo-Burmese border, so they also had to look out for Burmese army patrols on the border areas.

Two months later, they moved camp again, still further into the interior and dangerously close to the Burmese troops.

Food was even more difficult to come by in the Burmese border villages. The Nagas who lived there were very poor and the Burmese soldiers took away what little food they had. The Undergrounds did not have the heart to ask them for help. But the villagers would themselves bring to them, time and again, wildlife they had found in their traps for that was abundant in these areas. In all these gestures that attempted to ease their hardships a little, a bonding was created.

They continued to train in jungle survival and warfare, the veterans teaching the younger men how to decipher animal tracks and human tracks. They were trained at picking up scents. "You can smell an Indian soldier from afar," said one of the men to Mose. "Sometimes it's a food smell and other times it can be a musky body smell, but you learn to smell the enemy when they come close enough."

"What do you do then?" one of the recruits asked.

"Freeze and drop to the ground. Wherever you are, stop and lay still. Squat under a tree or behind one. He might just pass you by without detecting that you are around. As a matter of fact, that has happened to me twice."

The men grew adept at survival skills in the woods. Their priorities were in this order: concealment, food and rest. Their movements however, did not go unnoticed. The Burmese army was alerted and there were a few skirmishes between the Naga groups and the Burmese soldiers. None were from Mose's group. Nevertheless, all the groups received orders not to move about in the day.

Back in Kohima, the year 1961 did not end uneventfully. Loud cries woke up the whole village one night. There was a bright orange glow coming from the direction of the southern villages.

"They're attacking Jakhama!" someone shouted.

"No! That's not possible!"

Jakhama was the main army cantonment. They could see the orange glow spread and throw up a bright light in which they saw houses aflame.

"It is true! The military camp is on fire!"

The whole village watched as the explosions sounded and the fire burned on.

"Oil drums, most likely, or ammunitions," said one of the men.

They saw men running around like ants. They could not hear them from this distance, but the neighbouring villages later reported that the soldiers had screamed, "We're being attacked, take cover!"

The adults among them watched the fire fearfully. Surely it was the Undergrounds who had done it. What new and terrible repercussions would it have?

"As though life is not harsh enough," one of the women mumbled.

No one made any reply. They understood one another well enough.

There was little sleep for the villagers that night. They knew something as major as this would bring soldiers to every door to check for Underground members.

All over town, the next day's talk was about the previous night's fire. Then in the middle of the day, some interesting news came.

"It was an accident. Some jawan threw a cigarette too close to the ammunition dump."

One of the villagers had found that out from Naga workers at the camp.

The mystery of the Jakhama camp fire was never properly solved. The army stuck to its story that it had been attacked by the Undergrounds for a long time.

STATEHOOD

In 1963 the dismal news that Nagaland was being made into a state in India came as a shock to all in the Underground. It was not welcome news. Something had gone terribly wrong. Mose and Neituo didn't understand it. Their leaders were very angry. But theirs was a small camp isolated from the other groups, and they had no high-ranking officers with them.

"This is not what we have been fighting for. We don't want to be a state in India. We don't want anything to do with India," Neidelie, a senior officer was shouting.

"Who is behind this? Find them and execute them. They are traitors, all traitors should be eliminated!" shouted another officer.

"No," an older man cautioned. "Too much blood has already been shed. Let us wait and see what will happen. The works of those who lied will perish with them."

The camp was divided between those who wanted to go back to Kohima immediately and stop the statehood preparations and those who cautioned against taking any action. Serious debates started up spontaneously on the matter. Every now and then, the older members had to remind the others to lower their voices, because the subject was such an emotional one and their passion often overpowered the speakers making them raise their voices quite unconsciously. Towards the end of the day, the ones who advised caution had won the argument and persuaded the others to wait and see.

The new government moved swiftly to use both threat and persuasion to disband the Underground. Money and land was offered for the rehabilitation of those who surrendered and joined hands with the new government to build up the state. Very few jumped at that. The majority of the Underground members stayed on with the organisation, vowing to fight until Nagaland was free.

The cease-fire that had been talked of for a long time finally came at the height of the fighting between the Indian army and the Naga Underground. The Peace Mission, where the Rev. Michael Scott, Jayaprakash Narayan, a Gandhian, and B.P.Chaliha, Chief Minister of Assam worked with the local people, had successfully brokered peace. For a few months, there was some respite from the fighting. But the army continued to raid villages and torture villagers in the interior. The raping of women continued unabated. The Peace Mission received complaints about these cease-fire violations.

It was around this time that Mose was sent news that his mother was very sick. The officers granted him his discharge. Neituo joined him and they journeyed back. In Kohima village, they told their clansmen that they had retired from the Underground and that eased off the curiosity about their status. It was well timed as it coincided with the offer from the new government so people assumed they had accepted the rehabilitation offer.

"I didn't send for you, son," said Vilaü on his entry.

"No Mother, you didn't send for me. But I am grateful for the people who sent me the message."

"I am not dying, son," Vilaü said a little defiantly.

"Well, I thought you would be happy to see me. What sort of welcome is this? Or are you getting surly in your old age, Mother?" he teased.

Vilaü had a tumour in her stomach which the doctor said was cancerous.

"Does it hurt a lot?" Mose asked.

"More on some days. And with certain movements," she replied.

"I will take care of you, Mother. Don't worry, you will get better."

But both of them knew she was not going to get better.

On Mose's first days at home, he slept fitfully. He would wake up because of the unaccustomed sounds. And then lie awake from the silences. He missed the sounds of the jungle. His mother said he looked gaunt and needed to eat well, which he did. He could not get over the joy of eating food cooked by his mother. But she steadily grew weaker in the following months.

Sometimes she spent half the day in bed, getting up with difficulty to cook food. Mose pleaded with her to lie in bed, saying he could cook. But she insisted that it was the only thing that gave her some joy.

"How long do you think I have left son?" she asked bluntly one day. Mose looked at her and said, "Would you rather know?"

"Yes, much rather than not."

She was lying in bed as she was wont to do so nowadays.

"The doctor gave you a year at the most." Mose's voice caught in his throat as he said it. It was almost as though he were pronouncing a death sentence.

"I'd like to see you married before that happens, son."

"Oh Mother, I don't need to."

"You are at the right age now, son, in fact going past it. No one wants an old bachelor."

"I am 26, Mother, I am still young," Mose had to laugh.

"Well, it will make me peaceful to see you married," she argued.

Many things in the village were new for Mose. After all, he had been away for seven years. There were many more houses and new faces. The girls and boys in the age-groups below his were grown men and women now. Several of them were married and had small children. Mose felt like a stranger, and it took him a long time to slip back into the routine of village life again.

He learned that Neilhounuo, 'the rifle girl,' had left the Underground shortly after their departure. Curious, he and Neituo went to meet her. She was reticent about the whole matter and briefly mentioned a sick father. Neilhounuo's mother had died when she was seven. Mose felt stirred by the tall girl who spoke roughly and was visibly attracted to him. There was something about her straightforward nature that made Mose relax with her in a way he couldn't with other girls. And having both been in the Underground they always had something to talk about. Mose went by her house every time he was in the Tsiera locality.

Mose's choice of a bride surprised his mother a bit. Neilhounuo, the rifle girl. A good shot and a good soldier. But would she make a good wife? Vilaü wondered a little at that, but gave the marriage her blessing. There must be some good in the girl if her son had chosen her, she reasoned.

The marriage was not a big affair, mostly because of Vilaü's sickness. The newlyweds moved into Khrienuo's old house but spent most of their time at Vilaü's house. Surprisingly, they got along quite well, daughter-in-law and mother-in-law. As Vilaü weakened in the following year, it was Neilhounuo who nursed her carefully, washing her feet and massaging them with oil when she was too weary to get up. Neilhounuo made mild soups for Vilaü that teased her waning appetite.

One afternoon, Vilaü frightened them all terribly. She became delirious with a high fever. Neilhounuo never left her side and when Vilaü recovered she half-scolded, "You can't die now, Mother, you can't. You have to live long and see your grandchild."

"What? Are you pregnant then?"

"Of course I am!" Neilhounuo burst out and the two laughed together.

A BIRTH, A DEATH

Mose's daughter was born on the last day of December 1964, a big baby with thick black hair. Vilaü happily sat up in bed and held the baby. She named her Thejangusanuo but eventually everyone called her Sabunuo. The arrival of the baby seemed to give Vilaü more energy. She could sit for long periods looking after the baby and giving Neilhounuo time to rest or do some household work.

She really did seem to be better. No one suspected that the disease had completely ravaged her body. When her granddaughter was two months, Vilaü had another bout of fever. This time she did not recover. Her stomach swelled until she could no longer eat or drink anything. It felt as though something had blocked up her intestines. She could not get anything down. Solid food made her throw up. After a few days, she could not swallow fluids of any kind. She fell into an exhausted sleep at night, but woke up coughing. Neilhounuo ran to her side. She and Mose were keeping watch over her.

"It's all right," gasped Vilaü. "Can I get some water to drink?"

Neilhounuo quickly fetched her a glass of water.

"Drink slowly, Mother," she said.

"I will," said Vilaü.

She drank the water in drops, that was the only way it would go down. Mose fell asleep in the chair.

"Sleep some more, Mother," said Neilhounuo.

But Vilaü was wide awake.

"I think I have done all the sleeping I need to do," she said with a smile.

The younger woman did not understand at first.

"You should sleep, it will be a long day tomorrow," said Vilaü.

Mose, roused by their whispering, came to the bed and sat by his mother. He stroked her forehead,

"You're quite cold Mother, I guess your fever has left you."

"I think everything has left me son," she said with a weak smile.

Mose cried out, "No! Not yet, please Mother..." He frantically rubbed her hands and legs, trying to rub life back into her.

"It's all right son, it will be all right, my time is very near."

Mose's hard rubbing had no effect on her. She stayed cold and grew colder.

"I don't feel it son, don't bother," she said to make him stop rubbing.

They sat together, the son holding the mother's hand in his. They sat thus for an hour. It was useless to try and get any drink down her. It only made her cough and she said it hurt her throat.

Vilaü closed her eyes and sighed. And then she was gone. Mose and Neilhounuo clung to each other and cried as though their hearts would break.

The neighbours and members of the clan came to help the young couple bury Vilaü. Mose's clanspeople came and the community laid to rest the widow who had raised a son together with her mother-in-law. People recalled how she and Khrienuo had been so loving with each other, each so caring of the other that people forgot one was the daughter-in-law of the other.

"Do not reproach yourself for your years in the Underground," said Kezevinuo, Neituo's mother. "You went out to do what you had to do. She understood."

Neituo hovered around the house, supervising the burial, and looking after the details of the gravesite, planks for the coffin and everything else that was required to be done at a burial. His wife cooked food in their house for the grave-diggers.

Mose and Neilhounuo were surprised by the number of people who attended Vilaü's funeral. These were times of relative peace, at least in the village of Kohima. People wanted to honour the widow and offer their condolences to her son. Some relatives even travelled from Dimapur to offer their condolences.

That evening, Neituo and his mother stayed on in Mose's house and kept them company.

A NEW LIFE

Mose felt clumsy when he tried to be a father to his daughter. He didn't know what was expected of him. Neilhounuo would get irritated at him over the simplest things. One day, she asked in exasperation, "Didn't your father teach you that?" She regretted it the moment she had said it.

"Father died when I was two. I don't remember him at all," Mose spoke in a calm voice. There was no sarcasm or anger.

"I'm sorry, I completely forgot," she said in a low tone, "In my family, the men have always done that without being reminded."

Eventually they evolved a routine that worked for them. Mose's pattern of parenting was to be a "mother" to his daughter. He would think back on the way his mother had brought him up. Neilhounuo naturally became the strict parent. As their daughter grew older, Mose would say, "We have to ask your mother," if a difficult choice came up.

Sabunuo was a healthy child. At four years she was eager to go to school, but her parents decided to wait till she turned five. Neituo, who had married a girl from his clan, Thejaviü, had a son a few months younger to Sabunuo. Both sets of parents wanted their children to go to the same school. Neituo and his family lived in an adjoining house in his father's compound.

In the evenings, he came over as often as he could, to sit for long hours and talk to Mose about the old days. Neituo always had news when he came. Mose was amazed at the source Neituo's news came from. But then even in his youth he'd been an inquisitive boy often ferreting out news from other boys and enlightening Mose.

"They haven't heard anything about the group that left for China last year," he stated in a casual tone.

"That's serious," said Mose. "Couldn't they send out a team to investigate?"

"Too expensive. Besides, these trips take much longer than their first estimates."

"How many months is it since they've been gone?" Mose asked.

"About five or six months now, I think," Neituo replied.

"Hmm, it can't be easy to get news from Burma now that they have reinforced patrolling on the border," said Mose.

The Undergrounds who had left for China consisted of veterans and some younger members. Before they left, they had both been hoping to be selected for a similar trip but it had not happened.

"Seems they had fierce clashes with the Burmese army," said Neituo.

"That's not good," responded Mose. "If they waste their ammunition on the way, they could really run into trouble before reaching China."

"I suppose you know they are looking for more recruits.

Naga statehood means nothing to any of us. The freedom struggle is not over," said Neituo.

"I didn't know that about new recruits but I'm not surprised. Statehood is not an answer everyone is going to accept quietly," said Mose.

Neilhounuo came out with two cups of red tea but left the men alone to their 'man-talk' as she called it. Sabunuo was already asleep. However, Neilhounuo did not join the men on the porch. It was a deliberate choice. She smiled wryly as she remembered her nickname in the Underground. 'Rifle girl' they had called her, because she was so good with guns. She had been a better shot than the boys. But with marriage, she had chosen to put all that behind her. If only some lasting peace would return to their land so that they could raise their children in peace! The struggle had now gone beyond its twentieth year and there was still no end in sight. At 30, she felt a little disillusioned by it all. Too many had died. Needlessly. India was such a large nation. It could keep sending its soldiers in for hundreds of years.

Twenty-one years without any respite. Or any lasting solutions. It was a man's war. If it had been left to the women, maybe they would have talked it over and sorted it out long back. After all, it was they who bore the brunt of the deaths of husbands, lovers, brothers and sons. On both sides. But women did not settle wars. It was unheard of.

The women's lot was to mourn their dead. And the very next day try to find food for their families. The women themselves didn't think that was very much. It didn't compare with the heroic things that the men did. They never tried to take any credit for looking after their families in the absence of male members in the household. Certainly, not many women had done as she had done. Taken up a gun. But that didn't mean those who had stayed at home had not done brave things. Carrying messages hidden in the folds of their clothing past army check-points. Sharing their food with the ones in hiding, tilling extra fields when they could, cutting trees for firewood, repairing houses and taking on the works of men. Not many remembered what the women had done to keep their families alive in those dark years. Because war was men's business, not women's.

If only people would actively work for peace as they worked for war. War was for the young, and only for short periods. It killed something in you if it was prolonged. This war was much bigger than an inter-village war, where another village could have intervened and made peace between the two warring villages. It was getting bigger than life, much, much bigger.

SCHOOL AND WORK

In 1969 Sabunuo began to attend the Mission School. It was closer to home than Mose's old school. Her mother fetched her from school for the first two years. After that she was quite confident about getting to and fro on her own. Strong-willed as a child, she did not want to study those subjects that were tough for her. Mose sat patiently and helped her. He used different methods to illustrate things, to make her studies more interesting.

"Why don't you come and teach at our school?" she asked.

"Why? Are they running short of educated people?" asked Mose with a smile. There were many young graduates now looking for teaching jobs. Mose had not studied beyond High School.

"You're a much better teacher than our boring old History teacher," said Sabunuo.

"Well, it could be because I understand my student better," said Mose, smiling at her. "I may be just as boring if I had to teach twenty youngsters at a time."

"No, you'd never be boring," Sabunuo insisted.

At seven years, Sabunuo's workload at school had drastically increased. Mose tried to help her as much as he could in the evenings.

He had been offered work as a Lower Divisional Clerk in the Deputy Commissioner's office. But Mose did not feel it would be right for him to work as a government employee. He chose instead to open a grocery shop which brought in a smaller income, but gave him a sense of independence.

Neituo found work as a night watchman in the Public Works Department. He worked in the night and slept when he got off duty. It became routine for him to stop by at Mose's shop every afternoon, and if there were no customers, the two would exchange news and chat. If a customer entered the shop, it was entirely natural for Neituo to serve him as he knew the price of every item in the shop.

"How's Vilalhou doing at school?" asked Mose when Neituo sauntered into the shop one afternoon.

"Oh, he's all right. Unlike his father, he actually likes to study, that boy," Vilahou ended with a laugh.

"Good for him! That will help him get a job later," said Mose.

"You, you were quite good at school Mose, you liked studying. I bet Sabunuo is topping her class."

"Not exactly, she scrapes through," Mose replied.

"Hmm, you don't think we swapped beds some drunken night? Sabunuo could almost be my daughter, and Vilalhou resembles you so much it's not funny," said Neituo loudly with a mock-serious look.

"These things do happen, you know?" Neituo continued with a twinkle in his eye.

There was an young woman buying salt in the shop. Neituo

was playing up for her benefit. She smiled slightly at the exchange, wondering if they knew she could overhear them.

Hesitantly she approached the counter. Neituo was all smiles as he took the packet of salt and wrapped it in newspaper,

"That will be three rupees, young lady," he said as he handed it to her. The young woman fumbled with the change and gave him a five-rupee note. He was reaching behind the counter to give her change when she said, "You can give me two packets of matchboxes instead."

When she had left the shop, Neituo waited for about three minutes before guffawing loudly.

"You're not sixteen anymore, stop trying that out on the girls," Mose reprimanded him.

"Did you see the look on her face? Did you? That little smile she was trying so hard to suppress. Of course, she heard every word we said!" laughed Neituo.

"Possibly she thought you made it a habit to sleep with other men's wives," said Mose.

"No, she wouldn't go that far, we only insinuated that ever so mildly, didn't we? Ah women, such mysterious little creatures, never saying what they mean and never letting on how much they know," Neituo sighed.

"Oh, I have no such trouble with the two women in my life," said Mose. "Neilhounuo is very straightforward in her opinions. She's almost like a man, I say that in the nicest way. It must be her years in the jungle. She is totally unfeminine, yet I know she has a heart of gold. Sabunuo is a lot like her."

"That she is too, fine girl you're raising there, Mose. The credit goes to both of you, of course."

Mose thanked him and busied himself with stacking up jute bags against the wall in a neat pile. He would take them with him when he closed shop and re-use them. If he left them in the shop, the flour would attract rats. Mose was not restless as were some others who had been in the Underground before. Those men struggled to get back into the routine of normal life. No longer content with domestic duties, they kept in touch with friends who were still in the Underground and carried out dangerous errands for them.

There were three men he knew who had left the Underground and taken to heavy drinking. An old man of his clan commented on it,

"Men who cannot take failure turn to drink. But the struggle is not a failure, it's just taking longer."

The year ended with Sabunuo passing her exams and being promoted to the next class in the new year.

SPECTRES OF MORE CHANGES

Soon after that, three senior boys from Sabunuo's school dropped out of school. The boys went to join the Underground, but were intercepted and held prisoner by a group of Nagas who would not disclose their identity. They were half-dead when they were released. One of the three developed pneumonia and died. The other two were nursed by their mothers and sisters for many weeks. They were tight-lipped about what had happened.

"Break away groups," said Neituo in a half-whisper. "That's what is happening."

"Is that possible?" asked Mose. Mentally he began to calculate. Twenty-six years since the struggle had begun. They both knew about the rumblings in the Underground with new members coming in. But they could never have imagined the organisation becoming factionalised.

"Why?" asked Mose, feeling a little stupid to be asking.

"They say there has been some disagreements after the second trip to China. If you ask me though, it has been going on for a long time, and the longer India prolongs the conflict, the more we will see of this. They probably know that very well. Leaders change in any organisation, and along come people who want to seize leadership, etc. The Undergrounds have been to China twice. Of course, some of those who went have imbibed Chinese communist ideology. Don't you see that factionalism would fight India's war for her, simply pit Naga against Naga?"

"Surely, we would never go there, never turn so foolish," said Mose.

Mose found it incredulous but Neituo was always the more pragmatic of the two. They continued to be Mose the idealist, and Neituo the realist, as they called themselves. Much of the time, Neituo's was the more accurate perspective on the problem.

Apart from the unhealthy development in the Underground, the two saw other changes. There were new laws introduced in 1972. The Indian politicians had begun to tighten the noose after giving the Nagas statehood.

"We are not subtle enough," said Neituo.

"What do you mean by that?" questioned Mose.

"Well.. struggles like these are not for the rash. The armed struggle of the Underground can only do so much. In the end, it is the politicians who wield the upper hand and not the soldiers."

"You are being too subtle for me," said Mose."You mind explaining all that to me?"

"Come on, Mose, you know that the Nagaland State Legislative Assembly has passed the Unlawful Activities Prevention Act. That means the Naga National Council has been outlawed. The whole freedom fight is now reduced to a criminal activity. That prepares the way for that Indian General to 'wipe us out' as he says."

"General KV Krishna Rao," Mose said slowly. "Yes, I hear he also said that compared to Pakistan, Nagaland was nothing."

"And to prove that, they are getting the Disturbed Area Act passed. Which means the army gets immense powers again. Which also means that the army has abrogated the cease-fire terms. But who is going to listen to that? Especially when it is upheld by the State Assembly of Nagaland?"

"They can't possibly compare us to Pakistan. The problem is entirely different. The Indian army may have liberated Bangladesh but that doesn't give them the right to crush Naga freedom. The East Pakistan issue is completely different from the Naga issue."

Mose felt very sad about the new developments. He felt even more disheartened on hearing the news of the Underground. He didn't feel he could talk about it with Neilhounuo anymore. She would get irritable and snap at him.

"It was never an equal fight," she had said the last time they talked about it. "India is so much larger, we never stood a chance."

"But you were part of it too," Mose had tried to say. "Surely you still feel something for our struggle."

"Of course I do, I always will," she had quickly retorted. "But I now see it as something as foolish as disturbing a hornets' nest. If you trouble the hornets, they will always come after you. So, if they are in the middle of your field, you don't chase them away. You skirt around them and you leave that area uncultivated. Sooner or later, they will leave."

"That is a good metaphor," Mose had agreed. "But it's not

like that, Neilhounuo. India will not leave even if we stop fighting her army. She will claim our land if we don't fight. In fact, she has already done that."

"I do know that too, Mose. But how much longer can we fight? We should tell the British to come back and settle it all for us. After all, it was them that gave our land to India, didn't Phizo say that? Oh, this conflict is eating us alive!"

THE BOMB

On February 4, 1973 Ruby Cinema Hall was rocked by a bomb explosion. It happened during the night show. Screams and agonised groans followed the deafening explosion that made houses in the area vibrate. There was total chaos.

The explosion had destroyed the generator and people groped in the darkness, trying to find the entrance. Some who had carried flashlights tried to help the others. But most people were intent on getting out of the bombed hall as soon as possible. This led to a horrific stampede with seven or eight people jammed in the doorway and people behind them trying desperately to push their way out. Finally someone turned sideways and got out the door. The others followed suit and cries went up, "Don't push! We can all get out if you stay calm. Don't push!"

After some time, when people realised that no other explosions had followed the first one, they calmed down a little and scrambled out to safety.

The fire brigade and the police arrrived late. They were unprepared for such an emergency. The uninjured helped the injured to the hospital. Blood was splattered on the walls and on the floor. A young boy died in the explosion. He was one of the twelve-year-old boys who had gone to watch the movie without their parents' permission.

The hospital was ill-equipped to treat the injured. Doctors were roused from their homes and emergency operating tables set up to treat the mangled victims.

Mose had rushed down with Neituo to take a look. They tried to be of some help, but it seemed all the wounded had been taken care of. Mose made his way inside to look at the damage, knowing a little about explosions from his training. Though they had seen gruesome sights in the war, he was shocked by the sight before him.

Charred wood splinters from chairs lay strewn about and pieces of human flesh were everywhere. Suddenly he heard a whimper. Following the sound he found a young boy no one had noticed in the confusion. He immediately saw that the boys' legs had been blown off below the knees.

"Help me, someone help me, I can't get up."

Without any hesitation, he picked the boy up and carried him to the ambulance. One leg dangled uselessly, still attached by some tendons. Mose avoided looking at the bloodied limb.

Even though the fire brigade had arrived, neighbours with their buckets of water were walking around putting out small fires. As it was the dry season, they didn't want to take any chances. Policemen combed the dark interior for more bodies. Another young boy was reported missing. However, it turned out that he had felt sick and left early. He was safe at home.

"It's terrible, why would anyone do this?" asked Mose.

"It is terrible and not at all the right way to go," said Neituo.

"Do you know who did it?" asked Mose.

"No, no of course not," said Neituo vehemently, "I just have my suspicions, that's all."

The Naga Underground was held responsible for the blast and there was widespread condemnation in *The Statesman*, Calcutta. The explosion resurrected the fear that people had lived with in the mid-50s.

Curfew was clamped down once again and each house in the town was searched. Parents forbade their teenaged children to go out after dark.

Ruby Cinema Hall was not just a movie hall. This was where Kohima schools organised all their annual functions and variety entertainment evenings. In winter the up and coming rock bands liked to hold noisy concerts in the hall. A few weeks before the bomb blast, sedate ladies of the town had organised a flower show at the same hall.

"In a way, they have struck at the lifeline of the town, the social lifeline that is," said Neituo.

"You are right there. It will be hard to replace that. It has crippled social life," Mose replied.

"If that was their intention, they've succeeded," said Neituo.

"But who kills a bunch of kids to do that?" said Mose with anger in his voice.

"Yes. They could have found another target, or blown it up when it was empty. It makes no sense." Mose couldn't help feeling that things were going from bad to worse.

A NEW GOVERNMENT

"Should be interesting with this new government," said Neituo enthusiastically as he came in the door. He was referring to the newly elected Legislative Assembly of Nagaland.

"S.C.Jamir has been made Chief Minister. He has some new Ministers. It says in today's papers that Indira Gandhi is going to visit Kohima quite soon."

"Wouldn't that be dangerous for her? With her being the daughter of Nehru and all that history between her father and the Nagas?" asked Mose.

"This is 1974, not 1964. There will be a lot of security around her, of course. And, she is a woman. You know the Undergrounds have their own principles regarding women and children. They don't kill women and children," Neituo stated.

"I hope nothing happens, for all our sakes," said Mose,

"I don't like all these VIP visits, to tell you the truth. I don't know why they feel they have to visit Kohima. It only adds to the tension and we can do without that. What would they do if any one of their VIPs got shot here?"

"India wants to show that the Nagas are cooperating now. That is why it is important for them to visit and befriend whatever government is elected here," Neituo explained.

Neither of them had ever voted in the state elections. They were not alone. There were many villagers who never cast their votes. The memory of the forced elections of 1952 was still vivid in their minds.

"It's not our government. It won't work for us," said Mose.

"You are right. The people's hearts are not in it. It is still an Indian government with its loyalties to the Indian constitution," added Neituo.

"Phizo is right. In God's eyes we are our own nation. It can't be right to pretend we are Indians."

Indira Gandhi's visit, when it came, was widely covered by the Indian press. All the streets in Kohima were emptied of vehicular traffic. The Prime Minister of India rode into Kohima heavily escorted by army and police jeeps. The only sight the public had of the charming Mrs Gandhi was of her smiling and waving, as she was driven past assembled crowds. Sabunuo would always remember her clear profile and the shock of white hair above her forehead. She stood with the other schoolchildren who carried flowers and greeted Mrs Gandhi and waved happily at her as instructed. It was a whirlwind visit. Mrs Gandhi left very early the next morning without any fanfare.

Nevertheless, as Mose had predicted, the streets were tense and heavily guarded by the Central Reserve Police Force (CRPF). Rough, lathi-wielding police who didn't hesitate to strike down hard at anybody who looked like they might disturb the law and order. The CRPF had become a deeply hated presence because of the terror tactics they used against the public. Young men, inebriated or not, were regularly picked up by them and beaten until half-dead. The hatred grew and simmered.

One day Mose had a visitor in his shop. A former comrade from the Underground.

"Better not be late going home this evening," said the man.

"Why? Are you expecting trouble?" Mose asked.

"Well, the CRPF are looking for the people who killed one of them last night," the visitor replied.

"Hey, I haven't heard anything like that. What's it about?" asked Mose.

The man came closer to Mose and spoke in a low voice.

"Keep it to yourself, ey?"

Mose nodded his head.

"Some of my son's friends got so fed up of them, the way they are so arrogant and keep beating up people on any excuse. One of them used lead pellets in a slingshot which proved quite deadly. It hit a CRPF man out on patrol. Right through his temple. The man died. Since then, they have been on the rampage, looking for any excuse to pick on the locals and beat them senseless."

Mose was shocked at this. Both at the retaliation by the young men, and the information that a slingshot could kill a man.

"Are you sure?" he asked.

"You've not seen one, have you?" asked the man. "They're deadly accurate, in every sense of the word."

Mose closed shop early that night and headed home half an hour before his usual closing time.

"Thank goodness you're home early," said Neilhounuo.

"What's wrong?" Mose asked.

"Haven't you heard about the CRPF man who was killed? Everyone is talking about it in the village."

"Someone came to the shop and told me," said Mose.

"Well, it seems they are now targeting former Underground members," said Neilhounuo.

"Where did you hear this?" Mose asked.

"Neituo's wife, Thejaviü, has a nephew who works in the Central Investigation Branch. He saw a stack of confidential papers with lists of names. He says your name was there too."

"That's crazy. I haven't done anything unlawful after I left the Underground," said Mose.

"Our word against theirs, it never carries much weight, does it?"

"I can't close shop though. It would look even more suspicious, as though I had been up to something," said Mose thoughtfully.

"No don't close shop, that is a very bad idea. They would notice it immediately. Just go about your daily routine and pray that your innocence will be your shield," she said.

"The Lord will give me my due punishment if I have erred," said Mose in a rare moment of spiritual confiding. Neilhounuo was surprised. She had never known him to express deep faith in God before. It made her realise he felt vulnerable in a way he had never felt in his years in the Underground.

"You have nothing to fear. Yours was an honourable discharge from the Underground, and ever since that you have been a law-abiding citizen. They have no right to pick on men like you," she said passionately.

"We can only hope they see it that way too," Mose stated drily.

They both knew that former Underground men who were picked up by the army and the CRPF were interrogated brutally. Some had confessed to things they had not done, just to get the torture to stop. Neither of them spoke about those things but it was never far from their minds.

THE LIST

Mose felt tense for the next few weeks. Whenever he opened the shutters of his shop, it was with a feeling of deep unease. Would this be the day they came to arrest him, he would think and just as soon as the thought came, he would try and stop its course.

For four days in a row, he had felt watched. It was a most uncomfortable feeling. Quite possibly, his movements were being monitored and quite possibly they were watching the people who came to his shop. So he focused on staying calm, attended to his customers and did not encourage the talkative ones to stay on and chat with him. If they lingered, he would excuse himself and go into the back room and drag out a bag of sugar or flour and occupy himself with refilling stocks. That made them leave as they felt guilty about disturbing him when he was obviously at work.

Sometimes he would take a hammer and nails and make a show of fixing something in the back room. The loud hammering discouraged further conversation.

One morning, he woke up and decided that if they came to get him, he would be completely honest with them. There was a lot of peace in that decision. Gradually, things felt as though they had come back to normal, if it could be called that. Mose felt less stressed. He began to stop worrying and it showed in his face.

"Father's laughing tonight," said eleven-year-old Sabunuo when he had responded to a joke she recounted from school.

"Yes, dear," he said tenderly, "that was a really good joke."

They had not told her anything about the Bureau's name list. Not many people knew about it. Neituo and his wife, and their nephew, that was all.

Even back then, Mose knew that the day he had stepped forward to join the Underground, he had become a marked man. Though he had not been associated with it for many years now, it was apparent that there were people who considered him dangerous enough to be kept under surveillance. They knew where his loyalties lay. Men like Mose were seen as threats because they could be possible contacts between the Undergrounds and their sympathisers in town. In truth, Mose had never been contacted for that purpose. Not yet.

Mose was thirty-eight now. He was still sprightly enough to wrestle with the young men of his clan. The younger men laid bets on who would down him. He held his own against them, but he knew that time was catching up with him. He could not run as effortlessly as before. They could outrace him and he let them. His fighting days were over, as Neilhounuo had told him countless times.

The months passed without them hearing anything more about the name list. Thejaviü's nephew said that the officers had taken away the register with names in it. He wasn't sure where it was being kept now. It had not been destroyed, but was being kept in a safe place, he added. So Mose knew he was still under surveillance, along with some twenty others in the village. Neilhounuo began to join him in the shop. She came in late, but when she was there, she opened out the windows and dusted the shop and swept out the back room, raising a storm of dust and jute fibre for about ten minutes.

"Must you do that?" Mose asked, between coughs.

"It's because you don't do it frequently," she retorted, shaking out the jute bags till the whole shop was dust-covered.

"Now you've got it all over the counter," he complained.

"It'll soon be gone," she said as she finished the sweeping in the back room and came back with a duster.

It made Mose wish she wouldn't come so often to the shop. He was not usually untidy and had his own days for cleaning the back room, usually twice a month, but Neilhounuo wanted to clean it every fifth day. Luckily, it was soon paddy transplanting season and she became too occupied with field-work to get time to come to the shop.

Mose was left in peace to look after the shop, from which most of their family income came. He oversaw Sabunuo's school work in the evening. In the seventh grade, it had become more complex. Especially Mathematics. Mose considered getting her a tutor. It would cost a bit but he had to honestly admit that Algebra was quite beyond him. Sabunuo lost interest in any subject that she could not understand. Her teachers wanted her to concentrate on Maths for the next two school years.

"School is stupid," she said sulkily when they opened her books at night.

"Hmm, why is that?" Mose asked carefully. He began to think of a good answer to give her.

"Because I don't see how I will ever need algebra in my life when I'm finished with school. You don't use algebra to count how much money your customers should pay you for a kilo of salt!"

"No, you've got a point there."

"So, why must I study it then?" she asked sullenly.

"Well," said Mose, "Look at it this way. In one and a half years, when you are in the ninth grade, you don't have to take Mathematics anymore. You are a girl, you have the option to take Domestic Science."

"Yes, that is true, but I shall hate failing at Maths in my seventh and eighth."

"Listen, if you promise to work a bit, I will pay for a tutor to help you," said Mose placatingly.

"Would you really, Father? Will you have enough money?"

"Seventy-five rupees a month? I'm sure I could afford that for you," he said with a smile.

THE SHOP

In the next month, with the help of her new tutor Sabunuo's work improved. Mose and Neilhounuo praised her and that kept her in a good mood. Sabunuo had also found some girl companions at school now. She and Neituo's son, Vilalhou, had been inseparable until the previous year. Now they were both making friends among their own sex. They still met in the evenings to do their homework together.

In the meantime, Mose was trying to extend his shop. He worked two days to set up new shelves which he stocked with a few tins of paint. It was a more expensive investment than food, but it was not a perishable commodity, and it could stay on the shelf for many months. As a matter of fact, Mose was working on stocking his shop with a variety of goods so that his customers could get different things in one place. At present, no grocery store sold paint.

"Might be a good idea to stock kerosene too," Neituo suggested, "You know the Bihari labourers are always buying that."

Mose had to think that through.

"Bit dangerous if there's a spill," he said.

"True," Neituo replied, "but what's business without a little risk?"

He looked at Mose with his mock-serious face before his grin came back into place.

In ten years of shopkeeping, Mose had accumulated a group of regulars, customers who liked to walk the extra few yards to his shop rather than stop at shops which were sparkling new but impersonal. Mose's customers liked to linger over their purchases and exchange a bit of gossip with him. That was how it had been ever since he first started the shop. It didn't look like it would change very much any time soon. And while he hoped the shop would make a little more money, he was quite happy with it the way it was. Sometimes a new customer or two came to him. If they liked the way the shop was run, they came back again. Then they became regulars too.

Luckily, Mose did not have to pay rent for the house. It was an old shed which his father had built. It had a foundation of stone about three feet high. Mose and Neituo, along with some Bihari workers, had replaced the rotten wood and put in new planks. They had repaired it well. Then they had added the second room for storage purposes. The little shop was quite a solid structure now. Breaking in would not be easy. For one, the door, with its heavy lock, would make so much noise that it would surely wake the neighbours. Mose did not fear a robbery, but he was anxious about accidental fires.

As an afterthought, Mose began stocking some carpentry tools. Nails, screws, a hammer or two, odd planks of wood that could come in handy for small repairs. He found more customers from that. Neilhounuo suggested that he make a shelf to sell yarn too.

"I draw the line at that," said Mose. "This is basically a grocery shop. It's all right to stock paint and carpentry tools, but yarn? I'd be the laughing stock of the town."

But Neilhounuo insisted on it and Mose kept a few lengths of yarn in an inconspicuous place. Eventually she had to admit it was a bad idea because there were no buyers for it. The yarn gathered flour-dust and looked quite unappealing after a few weeks. Finally she took it all home one day, and after washing it out, used it to weave two body-cloths.

Neituo thought it was greatly amusing and teased Mose about it for months.

"Where's the yarn then? Have you sold it already?"

"Why do you want to know?" Mose asked. He didn't want to tell Neituo the truth because he knew his friend would find some way of teasing him.

"Oh, I was so inspired by the yarn in your shop, I thought I would take up weaving myself," said Neituo in a high-pitched woman's voice.

"Why, that is excellent news," Mose responded gruffly. "Here dear, you look after the shop while I go and find some wood to whittle a shuttle and loom for you."

Sabunuo began to come to the shop after school. Mose did not stop her. He liked her company and Neituo was better behaved when the young girl was around. The three of them went home together at closing time. If they closed a bit early, they could buy vegetables from the last sellers. The trio became a familiar sight, father and daughter and Neituo with his big bag. Sabunuo was very fond of Neituo, who would tell her stories and anecdotes that kept her laughing as they walked home.

VANDALS

One afternoon, Mose was alone in the shop. He had picked up the dustpan and begun to sweep up rice grains on the floor when two young men came in the door. Mose laid the dustpan aside and came forward to serve them. "Yes, would you like to buy anything?" he asked in a cordial voice.

The pair did not smile or respond to his query. They were both young men in their twenties. They wore smart jackets and jeans, and both were clean-shaven with close-cropped hair. The taller man grabbed a bottle of orange squash and began to pour it over the jute bag that held sugar.

"What do you think you are doing? Stop it!" Mose shouted as he came forward to prevent it. The man laughed and swung the bottle in Mose's direction and kicked at the jute bag. At about the same time, the second man started to throw the cans of paint from the shelves. He did it violently so that the lids on some cans opened and the paint spilled on the floor.

"Stop! Stop, you have no right!" Mose shouted again. He tried pushing the taller man out the door. The next instant, a fist slammed into his face and temporarily blinded him.

Lowering his head, he kept pushing the first man out. A second fist came at him and Mose struggled to clear his head. It was difficult to think straight now. Instinctively, he tried to protect himself from the blows. A third blow made Mose slump to the floor in pain.

As he was kneeling on the floor, the tall one called out,

"Traitors! You and your kind have sold out the cause. This is just the beginning. Next time it will be worse!"

"What are you talking about? I'm no traitor!" Mose shouted.

"We'll get all of you in the end. We have no pity for people like you."

"I don't know what you mean. You get out of my shop do you hear? How dare you threaten me like this?" Mose shouted angrily.

Just then, Neituo came to the door. The first thing he saw was Mose on the floor with a rapidly swelling eye.

"Mose! What's happened?" he cried out.

The tall one came between the two of them and placed himself in front of Neituo.

"None of your business. Unless you want a taste of the same yourself," he said in a threatening tone. It made Neituo back up momentarily from the unexpectedness of it. But Neituo, short and stockily built, was a fighter.

"Did you do that to him?" he asked, raising his fists, and throwing off his body-cloth in the same instant. He caught hold of the man by his collar and held him roughly, almost lifting him off the ground.

"Answer me, did you do that?" Neituo barked.

The man was too surprised to do anything. He saw his friend edging out of the door, trying not to draw attention to himself. Neituo saw the direction in which his eyes had gone and, only then, noticed the other man. He threw the man in his grip at the wall, and lunged after the other man but it was too late. The second man had run off, and his companion seeing his chance, half crawled to the door, got up quickly and sped away.

Neituo would have given them chase but Sabunuo's sudden appearance prevented him.

"Father! What are you doing on the floor? *Apuo* Neituo, Father's bleeding!"

Neituo came back to Mose and they helped him to his feet. He kept saying he was all right. Sabunuo was shocked to see her father bleeding from his nose and mouth. There was some water in the back room. She fetched it and Mose cleaned himself with it.

"Lie down a bit, it will stop the bleeding," said Neituo.

The men exchanged a look. What would they tell Sabunuo, that was uppermost on their minds.

"Let him rest a bit, dear, don't talk to him yet," said Neituo to the girl.

He was thinking very fast. How much could they tell her? If they hid the truth from her, would it endanger her as well? She came to the shop every day after school. Had she noticed the men running off from the shop?

In the end, they told her that it was two men who were trying to leave without paying and when Mose tried to make them pay, one of them let fly with his fists.

"It was so unexpected. If I had been more prepared, I could have taken on both of them," mumbled Mose. His lower lip was beginning to swell and it made talking difficult.

"Oh no Father! I don't want you fighting. We'll think of

something. We will get the police to frighten them off," said Sabunuo.

"Ah, we will handle it ourselves, you know how the police are. They'd probably scare off our customers," said Neituo with a small smile.

Sabunuo seemed to accept their story that the two men had tried to rob her father. Neituo cleared away the spilt paint and damaged bag of sugar. Two tins of paint were dented but unopened. They could be sold at a lower price. The sugar was unusable though. It was a half bag of sugar. Neituo put half in another jute bag and dragged it to the municipal trash bin.

Fortunately there was just one customer in the shop after that. Neituo served him and the man left when he saw that Mose was not around. After a while, Mose felt his head clearing and insisted that he didn't need to rest more. So they closed the shop and walked home. On the way, a few people they knew noticed Mose's swollen face.

"Mose, what happened?"

"Oh, I was doing some work and, clumsy me, I stumbled on a box of paint and hit my eye on the hammer, haha."

"Is it hurting? It looks terrible."

"No, no, it's not hurting. It just looks awful, that's all."

"If I didn't know you well, I'd have thought you'd been brawling."

"He he, now that would be quite a story, wouldn't it?"

REVELATIONS

There was no way they could hope to fool Neilhounuo with that story though. The moment she saw Mose's face, her face hardened. Mose knew that look only too well. It meant that she would not be fobbed off with anything less than the truth.

She ignored Neituo completely. Neilhounuo was not being rude, it was just her nature to completely focus on something to the point of becoming oblivious to other things or people around her. She made Mose sit down in a low seat by the fireplace. Then she quickly fetched a basin and mixed hot and cold water in it. The water turned light purple from the jentian violet she had poured into it. Mose grimaced a bit at the sight of it.

"It doesn't hurt, you know that," she said.

"I hope so."

Neilhounuo bathed his lip as gently as she could and cleaned his wounds.

"What did they want?" she asked bluntly.

Mose's eyes flicked to Sabunuo warningly.

"After supper then," she said.

Mose had trouble eating. His mouth smarted painfully when he tried to eat the hot broth. So he drank some cold milk instead. Quickly clearing away the pots and pans after their meal, Neilhounuo sat down beside him.

"Sabunuo, go play for a bit. Your father and I have to talk," she said in a firm voice. The young girl did not protest.

"I'll go do my homework now," she said and left them alone.

"Two men, quite young," Mose began. He didn't need any more prompting from her. She was listening intently.

"They looked mean from the moment I saw them. The one poured orange juice into the sugar and the other threw the paint tins to the floor."

"Did you use your fists first?" she asked.

"I guess it happened simultaneously. I remember shouting and trying to push the first man out the door when the fist came at me, right in my face."

"Mose, you do realise this was not an ordinary robbery? They were after something else, weren't they?"

"I know that. They were shouting, 'Traitors, you and your kind have sold out the cause!' They spoke in Nagamese."

"Which tribe do you think they were from?"

"Difficult to say, I was so intent on getting them out and after the third blow, I didn't think about what tribe they might be from."

"You could close the shop, you know," she said.

"What? How would we live then? What are you saying, Neilhounuo?"

"You're too easy a target if you are in the shop everyday."

"True. But we can't simply close shop and let them see we are scared of them. We haven't done anything wrong. Closing the shop will be just what they want. It will be playing right into their hands, Neilhounuo."

"Who knows how far they will go next time?" She said with a look of resignation on her face.

Neither of them slept well that night. Mose dreamt he was in the shop and the men had returned with guns this time. One laughed as he aimed it at him and pulled the trigger. Mose gave a little cry and woke. His cry woke Neilhounuo too. "Get rid of the shop," she said and turned over to sleep again.

The next day, Neituo came in earlier than usual.

"Just checking that you're not fist-fighting with your customers," he quipped.

Mose didn't smile and Neituo became serious.

"Those two, they were not after money, were they?" Neituo asked.

"No, that never came up at any point."

"Have you heard anything more about the rumblings in the Underground?" Neituo questioned with his head cocked to one side.

"No," Mose replied, shaking his head.

"It's a breakaway group. They are on the lookout out for former Underground members."

"Then, this is the factionalism we were talking about earlier?" said Mose.

"Yes, that's right."

"But why pick on us? We are no longer part of it."

"It's an ugly campaign. News has reached town that they have killed the Underground leaders in eastern Nagaland. The breakaway members are calling the others Shillong Accordist traitors. This is going to get uglier and uglier, I tell you, Mose.

We have no idea how many men have actually been killed by the factional group now."

"My God! Then – then we have played right into India's hands! This is what the Indian army would want – for us to fight each other and fight their war for them!" exclaimed Mose.

"Shh..." Neituo had to caution him. "We can't trust anyone now. Remember that Shillong Accord treaty that was signed last year? The treaty to stop the fighting which was signed between the Indian government and the captured Naga leaders? Now the Indian government has had to admit that it was an invalid treaty because it was signed under duress. Actually that was what the Underground maintained throughout. The Naga signatories were prisoners tied to their beds and carried to court in stretchers."

"Yes, yes," Mose burst out impatiently. "You mean to say that the treaty has been found invalid only now? Everyone knows that, or should know that because the day those men were released they immediately went back to the Underground and continued the fight. It didn't mean anything to us here."

"Listen carefully, Mose, I am saying that the Indian government has itself declared the treaty an invalid document. What we think is irrelevant, but if the Indian government declares it invalid, there's no reason to even consider the Shillong Accord as having any bearing on our destiny."

"That's brilliant, Neituo! Try convincing the two who came here yesterday with that," said Mose wryly.

"I know, I know, they just need an excuse to seize power, and this is a fine one," said Neituo.

"Pray it doesn't go further than this, it's madness, just madness!" Mose ended.

THE VIOLENCE SPREADS

Mose had no more visits from those two. But from time to time, strangers would come into the shop. They didn't buy anything substantial. A matchbox or a bar of soap. Sometimes, they would ask for something that Mose did not stock. But these men lingered long enough to make Mose feel suspicious of them. Their eyes darted everywhere, into the dark corners in the shop and followed Mose if he went into the back room to fetch something. Beady-eyed men. At first Mose thought that they all dressed alike, but after some visits, he realised it was not their clothing, but their manner that made them all look similar. Tense young men looking for something, Mose was not sure what, but he keenly felt they wanted to find it in his shop. It made him stop stocking anything that could be interpreted as a weapon. He took the hammer and carpentry tools home. He always kept the window open, so that he could see people passing by before they saw him.

Mose wasn't the only person being targeted. Some former members of the Underground received threatening letters calling them traitors and saying they would be eliminated.

'This is ridiculous,' they said. However, it made them change their lifestyles. Some of them were prominent men of their clans and the clans appointed young men to guard them outside the village area. Mose declined his clan's offer to give him some protection. "I'd feel safer if I were alone," he explained. He feared more reprisals if he were to be accompanied by bodyguards, and he didn't want any harm coming to them on account of him.

News of the killings of the Underground leaders had spread like wildfire. One of those killed was the young and intelligent Mayanger. Two years ago this charming graduate from the Ao tribe had been approached by the Nagaland government with excellent job offers. Parents with grown daughters were very interested in the young man. But Mayanger had rejected all that saying that he wanted to help his countrymen in their struggle. He joined the Undergrounds and they went east. Some months after he had left reports trickled in. Mayanger had tried to prevent the infighting, but had been taken prisoner and shot dead, along with the rest. It was a chilling story. A man who had given up so much and had been trying to reconcile the two groups, ruthlessly killed by the Socialists. People who heard how he'd been killed said that those who would shoot fine men like that would certainly not stop at anything.

"But why are they doing it? What will they gain by it?" asked Mose.

"Power, for one," said Neituo in a low voice. "This is a Marxist technique, rule the masses by terrorising them, you should know that, Mose. You are better read than I. The new group calls itself the National Socialist Council of Nagaland."

"But we are not Communists, we are Christians," Mose protested.

"It's not about religious beliefs, my friend, it is about power and how to seize it," said Neituo.

"That puts the whole struggle into a different light now," Mose stated.

"It complicates it, and in doing that, it destroys it," said Neituo grimly.

"Do you really think so?" Mose asked.

"I am quite sure it's the end of our Naga cause," Neituo responded, "When you begin to kill each other, you no longer have a cause left, do you? You have as good as destroyed your own cause."

"Hmm, then the Indian government has just been handed a very good reason for being here."

Mose suddenly felt tired, tired and old.

PART TWO

THE NEW GENERATION

"**D**id they have to shoot at students? Couldn't they have used tear gas?" Neituo was referring to the March killing of two students in a protest rally in the heart of Kohima town. People were very angry with the police for having used live bullets to quell the protest.

It all started when the Naga Students Federation called for a rally to protest against the extension of the Disturbed Area belt from 5 kms to 20 kms along the Indo-Myanmar border. The police who had come onto the scene of the rally were pelted with stones by some of the students. Panicking, they called for reinforcements and things quickly went out of control. In a few hours, two students lay dead and many more suffered injuries .

"What's happening to us?" the women were heard wailing on the streets of Kohima.

Mose echoed her words now.

"We" began Neituo ominously, "are dying. That's what is wrong with us. We are losing all human decency and sense of taboo. Human life is becoming worthless and utterly dispensable."

"But who would want that for our people? Our culture is not like that at all. We grew up learning to respect life. Taboo breakers will come to a terrible end, we all know that," said Mose, half in protest.

"Modern society has no room for the taboos anymore, Mose. It is just us old timers who think of things like that."

Mose had streaks of gray in his hair now. Neituo dyed his hair once every six weeks.

"Surely we are not so old, are we? I'll be forty-nine next month. And you are in the same age-group as I, Neituo."

"Forty something is old compared to twenty or even twenty-five. The cadres are all in that age-group. We would never outrun them."

"No. But we could out-teach them, couldn't we?" Mose asked unconvincingly.

The young cadres they spoke about were no older than Vilalhou, Neituo's son. At twenty-one years, he was working as a teacher at his old school.

"Only now am I grateful that Vilalhou has none of this rage in him," said Neituo in a confiding tone.

"And I that Sabunuo is a girl, though that did not stop her mother from becoming the 'rifle girl.'"

The last sentence made them both smile.

"How is my son-in-law then? Has he decided he wants to be a teacher all his life?" asked Mose. He used this nickname for Vilalhou only when he was talking about him with his father.

"Vila is not very ambitious as you know. If he is able to marry Sabunuo and have a regular job, he wouldn't want more out of life. He wouldn't know what to do with it," said Neituo without sarcasm.

"Well, our clan needs some men to be around to provide progeny and ensure that the clan will continue. We can't have every young man turning soldier," said Mose sagely.

Taller than his father, and leaner, Vilalhou had none of his father's fiery spirit, but he was a dependable young man. Though he had been greatly coddled by his mother, he had nevertheless turned out to be a popular member in his age-group.

"Why do you coddle him so?" Neituo had protested when Vilalhou was ten years and his mother still insisted on meeting him halfway from school.

"It's so he won't turn out like you and run off to join the Undergrounds," she replied.

"Oho, so that is what you are afraid of," laughed Neituo. "Don't worry, our son doesn't have it in him, anyone can see that."

Indeed, Vilalhou was uninterested in the freedom struggle in a manner that almost bordered on autism. He could work steadily at his job or fix things around the house. But beyond that, he didn't feel curious about the goings-on around him. Definitely not in the way that his father and Mose were.

When they were at school, Sabunuo was fiercely protective of him. Nine months older, she would threaten bigger boys who tried to pick on him. It was a funny love story. They never went far from each other even in their growing up years. Now the two planned to marry when Vilalhou had saved a little more money from his job. They were talking about dates and considering an end-of-the-year wedding.

Both sets of parents approved of it heartily and even pushed them to bring the date forward. However, Sabunuo was quite adamant that she would wait until December. Her reason was that she wanted to save towards her new home and have enough to start a household without burdening her parents. Sabunuo preferred to set up her own weaving business, rather than be employed by someone else. She was good at her work, and in a few months had already hired two girls from the Dimasa Kachari tribe of Assam. The girls wove woolen body-cloths which had a ready market in winter. Sabunuo keenly observed what woven items people used and she extended her weaving into school bags and table-mats, which the wives of officers liked to buy.

"They'll be all right, those two," their parents would say of them with a smile when they discussed them.

"Yes they have more sense between the two of them than us four," Neilhounuo remarked.

MORE KILLINGS

Sabunuo and Vilalhou were married in December 1986 in a very simple ceremony. That was how they both wanted it. No fuss. They settled into a house in Neituo's compound so they were close to both sets of parents.

Sabunuo transferred her weaving looms to her in-laws home and started work two days after the wedding. When relatives visited she would serve them food, but did not encourage them to stay long. Being a hard worker she did not like to while time away gossiping. In the early days of their marriage her conduct was misunderstood by them, and rumours travelled back to the family that she was rude and unfriendly. It hurt her more than she would admit. Her mother-in-law, Thejaviü, comforted her and said it would work out and that lies did not have a long life.

"Lies are like fire made from bad firewood. They flare up, but cannot leave embers. These rumours are like that. In time those who started them will be forced to change their minds, and if they don't we don't care for them," she said.

Sabunuo knew her mother-in-law was right. She felt very fortunate to have known her husband's family all her life.

Especially since she was nervous about the older women among her husband's relatives, who were now eagerly waiting to hear if she was pregnant or not. In the first year the young couple attracted much interest and attention. Was the wife showing any indications of pregnancy? This was a much discussed topic of conversation. Since Sabunuo showed no signs, speculations arose about her family's fertility. Somebody remembered a detail from the bride's family history about a barren relative and brought it to public memory. Almost triumphantly. Almost as though they were pronouncing a curse of barrenness on the young couple. Sabunuo was still flat-stomached in the tenth month of their marriage.

"Some daughter-in-law you've brought us, Neituo. Not only does she lack the common courtesy of young women her age, she seems as barren as a field in winter," one woman relative remarked to Neituo.

"Ah..she is a blunt one that one, but you are perhaps being hasty in thinking her barren. Let us wait till summer comes," he said cryptically.

Sure enough, when summer came, Sabunuo became pregnant with her first child. Around this time, a former school-mate of theirs was killed. That was the first factional killing in town. Shock waves ran through the community. He was shot in a hotel, and the terrified owners pointed out to the police the spots pierced by the bullets. One had killed its victim. Of the other bullets one had punctured a pot nearby and left a clean hole in the wall.

The killing paralyzed the town. "Why?" everyone asked. But they partially knew the answer to that. No one wanted to say it loud. They had heard rumours of killings that had been going on for a long time in the jungles. With this killing the factionalism that Neituo had named finally became visible in the capital town.

A few months passed by in relative quiet. Then another man was shot on his way back home. It came out later that he had had dealings with a factional group for some time. Vihu had been a part-time businessman who did contract work. He was killed on the main road. It was in the early evening, when most people were returning from work. Vihu was shot in the head and as he fell to the ground, the shopping bag he was carrying burst open. He lay sprawled on the road, face down and blood still trickling out from the shot that had killed him. Horrified, people ran off in different directions. His killer ran down the Mission road with his gun held high. No one tried to stop him. After some minutes a few men gathered round the dead man, and checked his identity. The police were in the vicinity, and they quickly came to take the body away.

His widowed mother heard that her son had been shot, and she ran out of her house in a mad frenzy. The vegetables he had bought lay where he had dropped them. Beating her chest, she covered the blood on the road with her arms and wept out loud, "This is my child's blood. Who has done this to my child?" The women of the neighbourhood came out to soothe her and escort her back, but she was inconsolable, and she let out choked screams that rent the air. There was hushed silence on the roads that evening. Car owners did not drive along Mission road where the killing had occured. They used the longer, more circuitous route instead. People walking past the bloodstained street, did so in respectful and fearful silence.

CRIME BY ANOTHER NAME

Four months after the killing of Vihu, Sabunuo gave birth to a boy. It was a home delivery with the midwife attending her. The baby was quite healthy, and named Neingusatuo by his paternal grandmother. Everyone called him Neibou. His father, Vilalhou was very pleased as were his grandparents. They were more pleased on Sabunuo's behalf because it put a stop to all the rumours circulating about her barrenness. Even when she was heavily pregnant, the same women who had suggested she might be infertile, had remarked,

"All right, so she is finally pregnant but it's difficult to say anything until the birthing is done."

The baby disarmed them all. He was an easy baby, smiling or gurgling at anyone who came near. As he grew bigger, Sabunuo laid him on a mat while she worked. He was quite happy to lie there, watching every movement of his mother, and crying only when he was hungry. Both Thejaviü and Neilhounuo liked to babysit him. But Sabunuo insisted that they not spoil him by carrying him too frequently, so the grandmothers would sit by him and coo to him. Occasionally, his mother allowed them to carry him while she worked. Neilhounuo would get the roughly woven strap-cloth, and bind the boy behind her back and take him round the village. He loved it and happily smiled at passers-by, making them stop to talk to him in turn.

Neilhounuo spent more time at home so she could be with her grandson. She thought of taking the baby with her to town when he was a bit older. He had grown quite heavy, and Sabunuo doubted that his grandmother could manage the trip to town and back on her own.

"Is it that or have I grown weaker?" mused Neilhounuo. She wasn't as strong as she used to be. She had to admit that she was unable to do as much as before. Mose was 51 now and she was 49. They had lived hard lives. She still tilled the field, but hired workers regularly because Mose insisted on it. They had sufficient rice from both fields, their own and from Khrienuo's field which Mose had inherited. Mose had planted two trees at the spot where his grandmother had fallen. They were full grown now, and gave good shade on sunny days. On a fine day when there was not so much work to do, Neilhounuo planned to take the boy with her to the field. It was good for children to be taken out and given wide open spaces to play in. The village had become crowded with new houses, and the old play square for children was muddy in the rains. Nothing like the clean air in the fields and a romp in the outdoors, she thought to herself as she planned for a suitable day.

Out in the shop, Neituo's visits dwindled. He had been having trouble with his left knee. An old injury that troubled him on bad-weather days. He liked to retell the story behind his injury to willing listeners:

"We were being chased by a platoon of the Indian army. It was quite close to the Chakhesang border. I was a good shot, still am, so I sniped at the officer in the lead. I saw him fall to the ground. That enraged his soldiers, and they rushed in our direction shouting curses. We ran helter-skelter and I lost my way in the thick woods. After running quite a distance I emerged atop a cliff, but I could hear them behind me. They hadn't spotted me yet. I couldn't see any other way to escape except to jump over the cliff. I decided it was better to jump than be captured by the Indian army. So I jumped. It was a long way down. I heard a crack as I landed on my left side. My knee had taken the impact of the fall and I went all stiff. The Indians were climbing down the cliff so I dragged myself to the shelter of a small cave and waited for their voices to retreat. It felt like forever, but they did leave. After that the pain hit me, ohhh.. such agonising pain in my knee and lower calf. I had cracked my knee cap and pulled some tendons in my calf when I landed. Oho ho, now that was painful – if you ever find yourself wondering about the degree of physical pain a man can endure, try that!"

September continued to be rainy so that kept Neituo at home more than he wanted. He still hobbled to work, but now spoke of early retirement. His knee troubled him with a dull ache when it rained. He tried a number of native cures, including wrapping crushed herbs around his knee and tying it securely. Sometimes it worked. Other days, he didn't seem to feel any different. Like this morning. Still he hobbled down to the shop. Mose was not pleased to see him.

"Shouldn't you be resting that knee of yours?" he asked in a rather menacing tone which was not lost on Neituo.

"Thank you for being so considerate of my welfare," said

Neituo sarcastically. "You do know what they say about old wounds, don't you?"

"What?" Mose rasped out.

"Well, they get worse if you coddle them, they are like old dogs or something," ended Neituo a little lamely.

"I heard different then," said Mose and they both had to laugh.

"Old dogs indeed," Mose snorted. "You really should be at home but since you are here, I suppose I should feel honoured."

"I..uh..er... wondered how business was going," offered Neituo.

"The same as before," Mose responded shortly and then softened a little, "actually no. There have been extortionists in the new row of shops. They haven't come to me so far, I guess I don't look rich enough."

"What did they want?" Neituo asked, "I mean, were they after goods or what?"

"Money, it's always money, and not small amounts either. They demand three, five, ten thousands. I barely sell that in a month," said Mose disgustedly.

"Who do you think they are? Faction members?" Neituo asked.

"Not these. They are just young opportunists posing as Faction members. They know that is enough to create fear in people."

"Fine mess we have here, haven't we?" said Neituo. It was more a statement than a question. "Political causes being abused by petty criminals for lining their pockets."

"Sometimes, I wonder if those young new soldiers in the factional groups even know what they are fighting for," said Mose in a sad voice.

"Cannon fodder. That's all they are. Somewhere along the way the cause was kidnapped and now it has metamorphosed into a mind game," Neituo responded.

"I used to hate it when Neilhounuo told me, 'your fighting days are over.' It was like she was pensioning me off before my time, you know. But that phrase is making more and more sense now," Mose stated.

Neituo looked up and raised his fists and said, "For these, their days are over, but this fight is not over yet, far from it," he said pointing to his head.

"That's where the real war goes on, isn't it?" Mose asked.

"Damn right it does," Neituo said in a firm voice.

"Remember when we tackled two of them in here not so long ago? Or was it all that long ago? Ten years? Ha! Has it been that long?"

"Twelve years, actually. I was thirty-eight or thirty-nine. Damned pup. Hit me on the nose when I least expected it. Had you not come in when you did, they might have done more damage," Mose recollected.

"Ah, but did you see they were scared too? They ran off when I threatened them. That's the trick. People should not be scared of them. They should fight back," said Neituo excitedly as though he had hit on a solution.

"That may work if they are not armed. Without weapons, no one is afraid of the other, but these days, they all carry a pistol which they don't hesitate to use," Mose stated.

"Only a coward carries a weapon and makes a lot of noise. A real man doesn't need that."

"In these times, do you think they care what a real man is? Do they care about honourable behaviour? Things are no longer what they used to be."

DISTORTED TRUTHS

"You two live in the past," said Neilhounuo when Mose was telling her about Neituo's visit.

"Anything wrong with that?" asked Mose testily.

"Don't misunderstand me. I agree with you but those boys out there, they don't have any idea what honour or cultural values are. They have no sense of taboo and probably never had parents who taught them any," she finished.

"That's a little hard to imagine," said Mose. "What parent wouldn't teach his child to respect human life?"

There were many issues they did not agree on and either quarreled bitterly or avoided confrontation by not discussing it, but on this matter they were in agreement. Neilhounuo was disgusted with the way the factionalism had created more crime in town. In addition to the bogus members, there were many jobless young men joining the factions and extorting money. They added to the atmosphere of fear that had become a constant in people's lives.

"They are nothing but criminals, and just want to live off the earnings of honest people." she said vehemently.

"You're right," said Mose. "But don't voice that opinion

outside these four walls. These are not people who would take criticism like that lightly."

"You know I won't. But one cannot help feeling frustrated at the way things are now. This is not what we wanted for our children or grandchildren," she said sadly. "I mean, we have had the war with India hanging over our heads all our lives. But to have our own men killing each other, and terrorising us is unbearable."

She picked up the body-cloth she was working on and went back to knotting the tassels. Their conversations ended like that ever so often. Frustrated and aimless dialogues. She had given up on the struggle long ago.

'See what it has birthed,' she would say by way of ending their arguments.

In a way, the increase of crime brought the vulnerable sections of the public closer. These were the people who ran shops and hotels and small businesses. It also included the office-goers who were affected when their salaries were 'taxed,' and twenty-five percent taken away by the factional groups. No one knew how to fight the wave of crime, because it was too easy to be targeted and hounded by the factions.

Neituo came early to the shop the next day. He spread the papers in front of him and paused at the headlines,

"Civilians support Insurgents in Nagaland," he read out loudly from an article in *The Indian Express*, a newspaper based in an Indian metropolis. The journalist had reported that the Naga insurgents actively received help from the civilian population who donated money to their cause. He flung the paper down in disgust.

"Why don't people come here and see the situation for themselves instead of writing such crap?" he spat out.

"Remember the war that is still going on here?" said Mose pointing to his head, "That is where it is headed. The Indian media is cleverly twisting the struggle into something else. No one is genuinely interested in ending it. Some people use it as a livelihood, toting a gun on that pretext and extorting money. Others such as this journalist here, use it to get a story in the papers. That's it, our great struggle for independence has been reduced to a mere story. You think anyone really cares about the people suffering on account of it?"

"No, of course not, why should they care? It's so much easier to sit at their typewriters and write out reports that they haven't verified," said Neituo.

He picked up the paper and scanned it, reading it with renewed interest.

"Ha! There's a story here about a jawan who went berserk and shot his officer. I must buy a copy of the paper tomorrow to see if there's a follow-up on that story."

"That's the second time that has happened, hasn't it?" Mose asked. "The first time was a jawan shooting his mates. Some months ago. It was a young soldier who was returning from a Northeast posting, if I recollect it rightly."

"It's not surprising. Think of the psychological damage they undergo when they have seen what we have seen. People killed like cattle, the same people they had been told were their fellow citizens. It must leave them with a terrible weight on their conscience afterwards."

THE RASHTRIYA RIFLES
ATTACK AND AFTER

The 5th of March 1995 was a Sunday. After the morning services, people went home to eat a leisurely Sunday lunch. Suddenly the quiet of the afternoon was shattered by the sound of gunfire. It went on for a long time. What could it be? Where was it? What was happening?

In the village, an old man who had stepped out of his house was grazed by a bullet in the calf. There was growing panic over the gunfire as the news spread that the army was shooting at pedestrians.

An army convoy was parked below the Japfü Hotel and the soldiers were shooting at everything that moved. They set up 3-inch mortars and also shot off rocket propelled grenades and 52 mm mortars into the heavily populated civilian areas.

One of the 2-inch mortar shells exploded in the front yard of a Lotha gentleman named Vandanshan. The exploding shells severely injured two of the daughters and their grandmother.

The horror-stricken family were helped into the jeep and Vandanshan drove his family to the hospital. On the way, the soldiers who had caused their injuries stopped them and questioned them over and over, delaying them from getting to the hospital. When they finally reached hospital, three-year-old Soyingbeni was declared dead and young Rebecca never fully recovered from her wounds. Her left hand and leg became paralysed.

The army convoy belonged to the 16 Rashtriya Rifles. The convoy was on its way to Dimapur after a posting in Imphal. There were as many as 63 vehicles in the convoy. The soldiers claimed they had been shot at when they were leaving the town area. But the story that came out later was that one of the tyres of the army truck in the lead had punctured loudly. Thinking they were being ambushed, the convoy launched their attack on the townspeople. For more than two hours they terrorised the civilians who were making their way home and held people at gunpoint. Reports came in that civilians were being stripped and beaten by the soldiers. The Chief of Police rushed to the spot. He started a long negotiation before the soldiers relented to his authority.

It felt like an eternity until calm was restored in the town and the shooting stopped. The silence did not last long. Soon they heard the sounds of mourning for the dead. In all, seven civilians had been killed and twenty injured by the firing.

The incident left the town badly shaken. "My God, we are not safe anywhere, not on our streets, not in our own homes, not from any one side," cried an old woman who saw the injured being admitted to hospital after the carnage. She was right. The Justice Sen Commission's report which came out in April, stated that the Rashtriya Rifles had fired 1700 small arms and 9 rocket-propelled grenades and 52 mm mortars into a civilian area. This time civil rights groups and human rights groups raised the issue vociferously.

The Rashtriya Rifles incident was followed by a series of talks between the Indian Government and the Naga Underground. Two years later, both groups agreed to a cease-fire. It began with what was referred to as the peace-talks. But three years on, the talks failed to yield anything concrete.

"I don't like this present ceasefire between India and Nagaland. Something wrong about the way it is getting so drawn out. It's like neither group wants to come to an agreement with the other's conditions. They keep bargaining without really getting anywhere," said Mose.

"I know what you mean," replied Neituo. "The trouble with the peace talk is that the Indians are still insisting on a solution within the Indian Constitution. It does make one doubt the sincerity of the talks. I suspected it was a pacifying tactic right from day one. Besides, when they started out, the Indian government made the ceasefire with only one faction, the National Socialist Council of Nagaland (IM) and ignored the others. They should have known better than to leave out the other factions. If they were sincere about it that is."

"You're right. They are not coming to any agreement yet and it's already three and a half years into the talks. It's farcical the way they keep extending the cease-fire year after year."

"That's the whole purpose of it. To keep gaining more time during which the conflict gets so irretrievably complex there is no way of solving it," Neituo ended.

THE AFSPA

In September the following year a young father returning home late at night was shot dead by an Indian soldier. There was a huge protest at the shooting. The victim was not a member of any faction and nothing illegal was found in his possession.

The Army sought protection from legal charges under the Armed Forces Special Powers Act (AFSPA). They claimed that the man had acted suspiciously by not stopping when he was ordered to halt. Under the AFSPA, the soldier who fired the shot was immune from being charged by a court of law.

The family and clan of the murdered man could do nothing about it. A protest rally was held by the public and speeches were made condemning the killing. There was nothing forthcoming from the state government nor was anything expected.

"It is just an excuse for the army to kill us, that is all that the AFSPA does. Why don't we join the Manipuris? They have been protesting for a long time to have it lifted, and their women are the ones forming the backbone of the struggle," said Neituo.

"Maybe something like this will unite our people," Mose remarked. "Have the Manipuris made any headway?"

"Not that I know of. One just reads about it in the papers, but I must say it's very brave of their women to spearhead it. The young activist Irom Sharmila, is already one year into her hunger fast. You know that she was arrested and charged with 'attempt to commit suicide'? That's all the government can come up with. I have such admiration for the Manipuri women. They keep at it stubbornly, which is their great quality. As for us, we make a great fuss at the beginning and then if nothing happens we let it die down. Things need to be sustained in order to work."

"Indeed they do, but they need to be sustained in the right spirit. No one can accuse us of not sustaining our freedom struggle."

"No, but somewhere along the way it has lost its 'right spirit' as you call it. Still, the government cannot use it as an excuse to rob us of all our human rights."

A customer came into the shop to buy flour. It temporarily stopped their conversation. It was a Bihari labourer. Neituo spoke to him in mock-Bihari, imitating the highly tonal dialect used by the workers in Nagaland. The man smiled broadly and joked back. Neituo handed him his flour and the Bihari folded his hands in a *namaste*, called him "*Saab*," and left.

"Funny how not carrying a gun changes a man completely," commented Neituo, watching the departing Bihari. "Without a gun, most Indians seem quite okay. If that had been a soldier, he would not have salaamed us, would he? "

"Soldiers make terrible human beings," Mose stated.

"Power corrupts, they say. Well, I'd say violence corrupts completely," said Neituo.

Mose was quiet for a few moments and then he spoke again,

"By the way, I've heard that the Naga Mothers' Association are holding a rally to demand justice for the army killing. They might ask for the AFSPA to be removed," said Mose.

"Feels like we have been asking for that forever. The damnable thing is, these laws are almost impossible to remove once they are in place. It's also called State terrorism. What's more, these days you're just as likely to be killed by the factions as by the army." Having said that, Neituo abruptly rose to his feet.

"Leaving so soon?" Mose asked.

"No, no, but this sort of talk always makes me want to pee."

"Go then," Mose had to laugh

"The army has got to stop picking on innocent civilians," Mose began again when Neituo returned. "Remember that man who was beaten to death last year at his sister's house? Nothing could be done about it either, you know."

"Yes, I heard that. Horrible incident. In front of his family and all, really makes you wonder how they can do that."

"Didn't the papers write about the army outpost being fired upon just days before they got hold of the man?" Mose asked.

"Typical army retaliation. They never go after the guilty. They are too scared to. It's easier for them to pick up an unarmed civilian and make an example of him."

There was a shuffling at the door and Mose shushed Neituo. An old lady came in with a shopping bag.

"*Hou*! It's very dark in here, isn't it, Mose? I can barely see inside the door," she exclaimed.

"It's because you have been in the sun, *Anyie*," Mose spoke soothingly. "Let your eyes adjust to the room then you will see we don't have it so dark," he chuckled as he said it.

The old lady squinted her eyes and peered at items in the shop,

"Ha ha, you are right. I can see the things on the shelves now," she laughed.

"Sugar and salt, that's right, I will have a kilo of each, and some *dal*," said the old woman.

Mose measured out lentils and other groceries, concentrating on getting the scales right. When she left he looked at Neituo apologetically and said,

"One can't be too careful. The wrong words in the wrong ears and we are in trouble."

Neituo acknowledged the explanation with a look. He picked at a brown spot on the counter and suddenly swore:

"Why the hell is the AFSPA still in force if there is a cease-fire? That itself ·is proof that the cease-fire and the peace talks don't mean anything to the Indian government. It is highly insulting not to remove it. The Delhi government is playing with us now as it did in the sixties. Dangling carrots before our cart. But it will soon come to an impasse, mark my words."

"I think you're onto something there," Mose remarked.

"I can see it is getting more and more complicated, and that is to India's advantage. First, the factionalism destroyed our credibility as a movement. The sympathy we could have gained from the Indian people has also been destroyed by this display of disunity. And now, to add to it all, there's that horrendous report of the Naga battalions posted to Chattisgarh."

"Uh, what was all that about?" Mose asked, "I don't know how far we can trust what the newspapers write. Are you talking about the Naga battalions being hounded by human rights groups because they have been brutalising the local population? Is that true?"

Neituo shook his head and stated,

"It's shameful, but absolutely, shamefully true. They went amok and were raping the women and shooting the men. That's no different from what the Indian army was doing here in the fifties! Killing innocent civilians and creating a reign of terror. To think the Chattisgarh Governor himself asked for the Naga battalions to fight the Naxals, claiming that one IRB battalion was worth ten CRPF battalions!" Neituo was speaking quite loudly at this point.

Someone opened a window in a neighbouring shop and the noise made Neituo lower his voice.

"It's a vicious cycle that keeps repeating itself. The cycle of abuse. Those who are abused repeat their abuse on others. I've read that somewhere but have forgotten where," Neituo ended.

"Hmm, perhaps that is what is happening everywhere. The Indian army seems to be having its share of problems too. There was yet another report of a soldier killing his mates and shooting himself after that," said Mose .

They were both pensive after this. They sat together in silence. The sun had gone down and they could hear the neighbouring shops pulling down their shutters. They sat for some more minutes before they both rose to go home.

PART THREE

NEIBOU LEAVES FOR COLLEGE

"I'm leaving for Delhi tomorrow, Grandfather. Father's going with me." The speaker was a smiling eighteen-year-old boy. Smooth-cheeked and fresh-faced, he didn't look as though he was old enough to begin college. Neibou, Sabunuo's son, had been admitted to the Shri Ram College of Commerce in Delhi. He would take a three-year degree in commerce.

Mose looked at the boy in front of him and reached out to stroke the back of his head affectionately. He was especially proud of his grandson, who had turned out exceptionally well. A good student who had always scored high marks all throughout high school, Neibou was now ready to move away from home and start life in the big city.

"How time has flown. It feels like it was only yesterday since you started at school!" Mose exclaimed.

"It's many years since then," Neibou laughed. "It's 2005 now Grandfather. If I were still at school, everyone would think something was wrong with me."

"Your grandmother and I will miss you," said Mose. "But we trust you will do well wherever you are."

"Thank you. Have you ever been to Delhi, Grandfather?" Neibou asked.

"No, the furthest I have travelled is to Guwahati. By train. I suppose Delhi is much bigger than that?"

"Oh much, much bigger. It is the capital of India, after all," Neibou replied.

"Yes, I do know that," smiled Mose. "We studied that at school," he added.

Neibou smiled back, "Oh, I didn't mean it like that, Grandfather. Sometimes I have to explain things like that to Grandmother. Sorry, I forgot you would know."

Neibou was about two inches taller than his grandfather now. He had taken after his mother in height, but he had his father's mild manner.

"Once you have got a place to stay your Grandmother and I could come to visit you," Mose kidded.

"Oh, will you do that? I would be so happy," Neibou burst out.

"Oh yes, as you can imagine your grandmother will be thrilled about getting on a plane and flying to Delhi. She will talk about it all year to her friends and neighbours. Especially on her way to the field and back. I can just picture her, her friends would never forgive us you know."

"And I could take you both round the city and show you the Jantar Mantar and the Red Fort. All those places we read about in our Indian History lessons."

They kept talking in this fashion for some time. They both knew Neilhounuo would never get into into a car to travel to Dimapur, let alone travel to Delhi on a plane. She had never stepped out of Nagaland and had no intention of changing that now. Neilhounuo had a mortal fear of trains and planes, planes in particular, because she had seen one burst into flames during the Second World War. There was no way anyone would get her into any form of transportation.

"Will Tuobou be going to the same college?" asked Mose. Tuobou was Neibou's cousin, the son of his aunt and about the same age as him.

"No, he is in another college which is not far from mine, so we can meet sometimes. There are lots of Naga students in Delhi. I won't be lonely," said Neibou. "There's a man who is from the Ao tribe. He cooks Naga food and takes it around to the hostels for the Naga students."

"Amazing, what will people think of next? Yet that is admirable. So, all that this man does is cook for students and he is able to make a living out of that?" asked Mose.

"Oh Grandfather, there are thousands of Naga students in Delhi. I suppose he only cooks for hundreds on a daily basis. It must be a good business or else he wouldn't be doing it."

"Then you won't miss your mother's cooking?"

"I'll have to find out."

Mose walked over to the bookshelf and took out a five-hundred rupee note that he had hidden in a book. He placed it in Neibou's palm.

"Here, buy yourself a cup of tea and think of your grandmother and me," said Mose pressing his gift upon the boy.

"No, Grandfather, that is too much," protested the boy, "In any case, I don't drink that much tea, he he."

"I want to give you more, but business is not good these days," said Mose. "You know you should never refuse a gift from your grandparents. We are blessing you. If you refuse it, you refuse our blessing."

"Oh, is that so? Then, I will take it gladly of course. I want all your blessings!" said Neibou with a big grin.

Just then, Neilhounuo came in with tea for the two of them. Mose was surprised.

"How did you know he was here?"

"Well, I am not exactly stone-deaf you know," she said brusquely, and then changed her tone and smiled indulgently at the boy,

"Neibou came to me first and I sent him in here."

"Ah, so I'm not your favourite?" Mose teased Neibou.

"Sorry, Grandfather, there's no way you can compete with Grandmother." Grandfather and grandson exchanged a secret look.

Mose's attention was drawn to his wife bringing in the tea. Her hair was streaked with grey. Bent over the mugs of tea she looked all of her sixty-six years. Looking away, he caught a glimpse of himself in the small mirror that hung by the door of his room. He was even more grey than her.

At his grandmother's insistence, Neibou ate a full meal of pork and bamboo shoot.

"I will miss your cooking, Grandmother," he said sincerely.

"That's a good reason to bring you back home dear," she smiled.

After some time, Neibou took leave of his grandparents. He had not finished packing. As he went home, the two of them stood at the doorway and watched him go. They stood watching until he turned the corner and was lost from view.

AN UNEXPECTED
FRIENDSHIP

Neibou's new life at the Shri Ram College of Commerce did not begin well. There were a few students from the Northeast who were in the Commerce section, but none were from Nagaland. There were two girls from Dimapur in the class senior to him but they were always too busy with assignments. In addition, the senior students had begun a month-long period of ragging the freshers when he joined the hostel. Some senior students insisted it was a part of college tradition. But for the most it was just an opportunity to intimidate the juniors.

After class, Neibou was suddenly cornered by a senior who called him a *pahariya*, a hill-dweller. He had said it in an unmistakably offensive manner, almost spat it out. Neibou smarted at the insult and swore never to mistreat a junior when it was his turn. Stories he had been told of Northeastern boys being picked on and intimidated and sometimes even beaten up came to mind. He ignored the remark. When Neibou did not respond, the senior boy made a lewd gesture and said something about girls from the Northeast. He said it in Hindi but Neibou knew enough Hindi to understand what he was saying. *Badchalan.* Easy women. Neibou exploded. He rushed at the senior and smashed his fist into the boy's face. Their shouting brought the other seniors running up and some of them pushed Neibou to the ground and began to kick him.

Neibou was so angry that he sprang to his feet and was about to hit the senior boy again when the fight was broken up by two wardens. The other boy was bleeding from his nose as his friends led him away, and Neibou's knuckles were swollen and bruised. No one came forward to help him. He felt homesick and very lonely.

Neibou was not a fighter. He had never used his fists before. But the senior's taunting had pushed all his buttons. He still smarted from the insulting phrases the senior had used. The targeting of girls from the Northeast had become a big problem in the city and he had read innumerable reports about these in the newspapers. It seemed that girl students and working girls from the Northeast were victims of carefully planned rapes and sexual attacks and the city was becoming increasingly unsafe for them. Protests from the students groups and human rights groups had not made much difference. Some weeks later, Neibou read about the rape of a young girl from Manipur. The two men who had abducted and brutally raped her, dumped her at the hostel gate when it was over. It sickened Neibou to hear the senior suggest that Northeastern girls were easily available. So that was how they excused their sexual crimes, thought Neibou still seething with anger.

The spate of crimes and sexual assaults against girls from

the Northeast had continued unabated in spite of the fact that some culprits had been identified. In more than one case, they were let out on bail. It wasn't safe for the boys either. It was difficult for them to find accomodation outside the few hostels in the university and even there they were often singled out and insulted for their culinary habits, for cooking beef and pork. They were often targetted and attacked and Neibou now began to wonder if it had all been a mistake to come to study in Delhi.

The next day Neibou was standing in the queue to buy tea when he noticed a lanky young man staring at him.

"Find something else to stare at," he snapped. Neibou was not normally so rude but the three weeks of ragging had made him depressed and irritable. To his surprise, the other boy apologised,

"I'm sorry I didn't mean to stare. You reminded me of someone." The tall boy stretched out a hand, "My name's Rakesh. I'm new too." They shook hands and Neibou explained,

"I was so sure you were another senior waiting to pick on me. Sorry. I've had a rough time."

"I'm sorry to hear that. I can't possibly rag anyone. Luckily my height makes my seniors think I am one of their classmates and that stops them from ragging me," Rakesh confided. "What did you say your name was?"

"Neibou. I'm from Nagaland."

"Nagaland!" exclaimed Rakesh, "You're from Nagaland? Wow man! Wait till I tell my grandfather about this. He was there in the 60s."

"Really?" Neibou could not hide his curiousity. Yesterday's incident had made him withdraw into himself and he felt cold and most unlike his naturally friendly self. But when he heard that Rakesh's grandfather had worked in Nagaland in the 60s, he was immediately interested. Anyone working in the 60s would have had to be in the army or police. There had only been a handful of Indians in the government offices back then.

Cautiously, Neibou questioned his new friend. Rakesh said that his grandfather had been in the Police and posted in Nagaland between 1961 and 1963.

"My grandfather has the greatest respect for your people. You should hear him talk. He always says the years he spent in Nagaland were the best years of his life," Rakesh babbled on.

Neibou was surprised to hear this. It never ocurred to him that some Indian soldiers or policemen might have liked their posting in Nagaland. He recollected the stories he had heard from his grandfather, of the fearful days they had spent running from capture and torture. Rakesh's grandfather had to be a very different sort of man from the others, Neibou concluded.

In the following months, the two slowly became good friends. They made an odd pair; Rakesh with his angular face and long legs, and Neibou who was shorter and had more muscle on him. Rakesh was thin-faced and always looked hungry. It was quite in keeping with his image that he also possessed a voracious appetite. Their favourite hang-out was the tea-stall where the man everyone called Uncle Ramu, served them tea and samosas. They frequented the stall so often that Ramu would give them a knowing look and serve them tea without waiting for them to place their orders. The shop stayed open late as it was used to serving a student clientiele. Ramu seemed to be there all the time. The light from the little stall was the last thing Neibou saw from his window before he went to sleep. In the morning, the shop would open early and they would see Ramu as they made their way to college.

Sometimes, Neibou saw two little girls playing near the tea-stall. These were Ramu's daughters. They called him *Baba*. Ramu was a short, swarthy man in his forties. He was a likeable man with a ready smile. Students thought he was almost as old as the college itself but in reality he'd been around for fifteen years. Old students spoke of him affectionately and he remembered most of them. He would give them credit if they had no money to pay or if their money was delayed. Most paid him back but there were some who'd left the college without paying him. Still, it did not shake his faith in humanity,

"Destiny will deal with them," he often said. "What will they get out of cheating a poor man? I feel sorry for them."

When it was late winter in Delhi, the two friends found themselves spending more time at the tea-stall, trying to warm themselves with cup after cup of Ramu's sweet, ginger-flavoured tea. Sometimes, he felt sorry for them and served them a free cup. The following week, the college had a two-day holiday, but it wasn't long enough to make a trip anywhere worthwhile.

"Next time, let's go to my parents in Haryana," Rakesh suggested.

"Sounds interesting," Neibou responded without much enthusiasm.

"You will like it," said Rakesh reassuringly. "It's quieter than Delhi. People are not so intrusive."

"I'm sure I will like it then," Neibou agreed.

It would be nice to get out of Delhi, thought Neibou. Even

for four or five days. Sometimes he felt so tired of the stares from strangers on the road. And the regular bickering with rickshaw pullers every time he went to the market. Local boys had twice insulted him to his face, calling him "meat-eater". A few days respite from all that would be very nice indeed.

ABOUT GRANDFATHERS

Neibou had not immediately told Rakesh about his grandfather. It was some time before he stated that their two grandfathers had possibly fought against each other in the 60s. The idea fascinated Rakesh.

"Why didn't you say anything before?" he asked.

"Well, I wasn't sure, I guess," said Neibou stumbling a little. He didn't want to admit that he feared prejudice and stereotypical thinking if Rakesh found out his grandfather had played an active role in the Naga resistance.

"But that is silly. It's not as though they are still fighting." Rakesh laughed and continued. "In any case, I have told you my grandfather has nothing but admiration for your people."

"Yes, you told me that," said Neibou.

"We must arrange for them to meet," said Rakesh enthusiastically.

"Er.. I'm not sure that would be so easy," Neibou responded. He was thinking back to some of the things his grandfather used to tell him. Stories of people who had died of military torture. He wasn't sure his grandfather would want to meet an old Indian soldier. Oh well, Rakesh's grandfather had been a policeman. That was a little different from being in the regular army, Neibou thought.

Rakesh was very eager to hear all about Mose. Neibou tried to tell him all that he knew. They had a laugh over the flag-hoisting adventure of Mose so many years ago.

"He must have been a daredevil to volunteer for such a job," said Rakesh. That made Neibou smile to himself because, try as he would, he could not imagine his grandfather as a tough young soldier, especially now with his hair completely gray and his back slightly bent from old age.

"Well, he's certainly not one now," he said quickly.

"Still, consider what lives they have led, these two, one fighting for freedom and the other thinking that he was fighting to preserve the integrity of his nation," stated Rakesh with a dreamy look in his eyes.

"Sounds very romantic now, but Grandfather doesn't tell it that way," said Neibou.

"How does he tell it then?" Rakesh asked curiously.

"Well, I mean, he does romanticise a bit too, but he also remembers starving and sharing vegetables that they found in people's fields, a gourd that they cut open and ate raw, or the time they found a rice field and plucked off heads of paddy, husked it in their hands and ate it, things like that. Of course, when he tells us these tales, he is proud as a peacock, you can see it in his face." They both laughed.

"Grandfather also told me Grandmother was so good at handling rifles, they called her 'the rifle girl'," Neibou added.

"Really? It sounds like a bollywood movie. Remember there was a movie like that, what was it called, Pistolwali?

Or Bandit Queen? Surely you know it?" said Rakesh in great excitement.

"Riflewali I think. However, Grandmother wasn't a bandit. We are not allowed to call her 'rifle girl'. No one is, not even Grandfather."

"The whole thing is almost like a movie, our grandfathers fight in the same war, they both survive and forty years later, we meet each other and become friends. What a plot!"

"Forty-nine years ago, to be precise," said Neibou.

"OK, forty-nine. It is one of those things that are stranger than fiction, you know," Rakesh insisted.

"Yeah, I know," said Neibou. "It is sad though that the war is still going on, even if it is in another dimension."

After a pause Rakesh spoke up,

"I, for one, would like to meet your grandfather."

"And I, for one, would like you to meet him," Neibou offered.

"Right, that's agreed upon then," said Rakesh cheerily. "In the *puja* holidays, I'm travelling with you to Nagaland and next holidays, you are coming home with me to meet my grandparents because they are visiting us."

"Hey, hold on a minute, what makes you think they would want to meet me?" Neibou protested.

"Oh, I have ways and means of finding out and I know that Grandfather is very eager to meet you," said Rakesh with a gleam in his eye.

Classes resumed the next day and the two friends were too swamped with assignments and classes to make further plans. Shri Ram College of Commerce was one of the most prestigious colleges of Delhi University. The students were hard-pressed with weekly assignments.

In a couple of weeks, Delhi came out of the harsh winter season and gradually grew warmer. Flowers bloomed profusely on campus, pansies and snapdragons in the flower boxes outside the college. The girls on campus had stopped wearing their long coats and boots. But they still wore cardigans because it would take some time before it got warm enough to go without. The rare showers that occured made the campus smell of grass and wet earth.

The famous ridge near Delhi University was growing smaller as slum-dwellers encroached into the wooded areas. Occasionally, they heard a peacock's harsh cry. But that was rare now. This autumn, there had been a number of crimes in the ridge area. Robberies and two stabbings. One of the victims was a Manipuri boy who had been robbed and stabbed. The newspapers carried the stories and some TV channels featured them. Worried letters arrived from home, so Neibou wrote back to his grandfather and mother to explain that they were not in the vicinity of the ridge, and that they were too busy studying to go out anyway.

HOLI

Neibou had met Rakesh's mother Dipti twice. First, when she had driven her son back to the hostel after one of the holidays. The second time, she had come to see Rakesh after his classes and she invited Neibou to visit them at their house. Forty-eight-year-old Dipti worked in a publishing house in Haryana and led a busy life. She promised to stay home for a weekend if the two boys could come for a holiday.

Holi, the festival of colours, was round the corner and Rakesh excitedly told Neibou that his grandparents had decided to travel to Haryana from their native Bhopal in Madhya Pradesh.

"That means you can meet them sooner than we expected," he added.

"Are they coming to Delhi as well?" Neibou asked.

"No, no, you are going with me to meet them," Rakesh explained. "You don't mind, do you? Holi is too short for you to go anywhere else. You can come with me and we will have a weekend with my family."

Neibou thought it over quickly and answered,

"That really sounds nice. But wouldn't I be in the way? It's a family occasion, after all," said Neibou.

"You're the reason Grandfather and Grandmother are travelling to us. You have to come. They really want to meet you," Rakesh pointed out.

After that there was no way Neibou could refuse. In any case, he was just as keen to meet the rest of Rakesh's family, especially his grandfather.

On the day before Holi, Rakesh's mother came to pick up the two boys. Rakesh and his parents lived on the border of Delhi and Haryana. Buses ran regularly, both the rickety country buses and the more well maintained deluxe buses. However, Dipti did not want the boys to travel by bus during the rowdy Holi period, when revellers were drunk and unruly. So she drove them herself along the long stretch to the Haryana border. The countryside was crowded with hovels by the roadside, or ran into scrub forests for miles.

Rakesh's home had a spacious yard in front and a bigger one at the back. In the servants' quarters, their old manservant lived with his family. They had taken to keeping a cow in the last two years. It gave a pleasantly rural touch to the compound.

When the trio had rested, another car drove up with Rakesh's father driving it. Alok, Dipti's husband, had picked up Grandfather Himmat and his wife Nirmala from the railway station. It was a joyous family reunion. Himmat was especially pleased to meet Neibou. He took both Neibou's hands in his and greeted him warmly. Himmat was a tall, gray-haired gentleman who was probably about Mose's age or a little older. Still holding his hand, Himmat led the way inside the house, asking to hear all about Nagaland from Neibou. Both Nirmala and Dipti insisted that they refresh themselves with some food before they began any conversation of a serious kind.

Dipti promptly served them dinner because it was beginning to get dark. Around the dinner table, Dipti talked entertainingly about her work and the people she met while Rakesh talked about college and the grandparents discussed their neighbours. Neibou and Rakesh's father, Alok, were silent listeners to the animated conversation. Neibou had discovered that Alok was a shy person and let his wife do most of the talking. Himmat, on the other hand, was a very curious person. He wanted to find out all he could about the boys and their studies.

After dinner came the sweets, traditional North Indian gulab jamuns were served. Juicy and golden these were delicious, floating in sugar syrup. Himmat drew his chair closer to Neibou's and said, "Now you can tell me all about Nagaland." He had a twinkle in his eye as he said this, which made him look like a mischievous boy about to open a big present. Neibou felt he could not help but warm towards this friendly old man with the kind smile. Himmat was not at all like he had expected him to be. Not stern and bullying like the Indian policemen he had seen back home.

"First, tell me where do your parents live?" Himmat asked. Neibou explained that they now lived at the Seikhazou colony, close to his grandparents' house, and that it had been some years since they had moved out of the village to live in the suburbs.

"Wait a few minutes, please," said Himmat. "I brought a map of Nagaland, let me fetch it."

When Himmat came back with the map, Neibou had some difficulty recognising places because it was an old military map. But once Himmat had shown him where Jakhama was located on the map, he recognised the hills and was able to point out the places he was talking about. Himmat's memory of Kohima was from the early sixties. He was amazed that there were so many houses in what formerly used to be Nepali settlements and cow-breeding sheds, or simply forest areas. He couldn't believe that Seikhazou had grown into a crowded colony of the Dapfütsumia clan.

"Your people were mortally afraid of these regions because they believed that evil spirits dwelt in these bamboo groves and took human lives. That is what my informers told me. They were ideal hiding places for the Undergrounds when they came to town," said Himmat using a pencil to point out spots on the map.

"This is where an army patrol was attacked by ten Undergrounds. They took away all their weapons. Now look at this ridge here." Himmat was pointing to a little protrusion on the map, some miles from Kohima. "Here is where an army convoy was attacked by a small group of Undergrounds. Three of them sprang onto the leading truck, shot at the group and went off before anyone could react. They were so good at using the surprise element."

Both Rakesh and Neibou were impressed at Himmat's knowledge of the Naga areas. Rakesh was so excited he kept picking out places on the map and asking what they were called. They went to bed quite late with Himmat promising he would tell them more the next day.

HIMMAT

"You know, when I got my posting to Nagaland in 1961, my friends called it my punishment posting."

"Why was that, Grandfather?" Rakesh interrupted.

They were sitting in the garden after breakfast. The women were busy cleaning the house and the men had been shooed out of the house. The men were only too happy to be left alone to pick up the previous night's conversation.

"A punishment posting is a posting to a war zone area. In the 50s and 60s Jammu-Kashmir and Nagaland were both war zones. There was fierce fighting going on in both regions. In Jammu-Kashmir, India had been battling Pakistani claims on Kashmiri territory, while in the Naga Hills, we were told the Nagas wanted to secede from the new nation of India. The additional information we were given was that they were primitive warmongers, with a fearsome tradition of headhunting.

I was Commandant of the armed 24rth SAF battalion. My headquarters, Madhya Pradesh, was far from peaceful. We were fighting dacoits every week. The region was unbelievably dacoit-infested and I welcomed a transfer. I didn't think of my posting in the Naga Hills as a punishment posting at all. But the troops in my battalion were nervous. They had heard so many rumours about the army being constantly engaged in attacks on Naga army camps. The army casualties were almost as high as the Naga casualties in those days.

I realised the importance of this next posting only when the Chief Minister himself came to send us off. We left with very high morale, believing we were going off on a mission to save the country. It was a very long journey, most of it by train and the last leg from Dimapur to Kohima by army convoy. We did not stop at Kohima, but drove directly to Jakhama where the Commandant received us warmly. On our part, we were relieved to see a very well fortified headquarters neatly arranged in typical army fashion, with barbed wire fencing the whole area off. Below the Jakhama camp lay the two small villages of Jakhama and Kigwema, quite close together."

There was a sudden noise from the kitchen. The maid had dropped a lid and it made a loud noise on hitting the floor. Himmat rose to attention, but then slowly relaxed and resumed his story when Rakesh explained what it was.

"Sorry, it's the soldier instinct in me, can never get rid of it. I react immediately to loud noise. Anyway let me continue... at Jakhama, a sumptious dinner was prepared for us and after dinner, we officers were hosted in basha huts. The basha huts were small huts made of bamboo with tin roofing, very commonly used by the army. The Commandant at Jakhama made sure we were comfortably settled in and it was rather late when we finally went to bed.

Our first night in Nagaland went very well, much better

than we had expected. After dinner and the warm reception we were ready for bed and retired to our own huts.

In the middle of the night, my orderly roughly shook me awake. I heard loud noises and ran out of the hut in my night clothes and my pistol which was the first thing I had grabbed. My orderly had the presence of mind to collect my luggage and my shoes. There was total confusion outside. Powerful explosions were going off every few minutes and I found the Commandant ordering everyone to keep calm.

There was a huge fire rapidly spreading to the basha huts. The fire lit the darkness and made it bright as day and we saw the flames leap quickly from hut to hut. Every few minutes, explosions went off and some people shouted, "We are being attacked!" We had our guns ready, but there was no sign of anyone charging at us. The fire meanwhile, had grown so intense it was not possible for us to go close to check for survivors.

Soldiers ran around with buckets of water trying to douse the fire. There were oil drums stacked in the godowns. Some of these exploded and the fire threatened to get out of control. Luckily some of the soldiers and cooks thought of throwing sand on the fire and they doused it in this manner.

It lasted about four hours in all. Afterwards, I failed to find my colleague who had been sleeping in the basha next to mine. With pounding heart we went to check his hut. We found his charred remains in the fire that had taken his life and burnt his shelter to ashes. I can never forget the sight of my friend and colleague, burnt beyond recognition. When daylight came, we somehow managed to send a telegram to his wife. Then we took care of his funeral rituals the same day. Oh, that was a hard thing! You have heard me tell this story before, haven't you, Raklu?"

"That's right, *Nanna*, but it's more interesting this time since I have gotten to know someone who is from those regions. And maybe his grandfather fought you at some point," Rakesh replied.

"Possibly," Himmat answered thoughtfully.

"Nanna, did you find out if the camp was attacked by the Undergrounds?" Rakesh asked.

"Well," said Himmat, "the Deputy Commissioner ordered an inquiry into the matter. But it was difficult to determine if we had been attacked or if a careless jawan had thrown a cigarette stub into the oil drum area. Our battalion moved to Mokokchung that afternoon. My troops were trigger-happy after the incident, and I had to keep warning them not to keep their guns cocked. We didn't want any more trouble."

"Did you make any friends amongst the local people, Nanna?" Rakesh wanted to know.

"No, we were not allowed to make contact with the local population at all. But I did manage to befriend the cook who was a Naga who had served in the Assam Regiment before. He was a good man. He told me a lot about the Naga cultural habits.

Our posts and Battalion Headquarters were situated on hillocks, fortified with bamboo fencing and panjies. Do you know what panjies are? Sharp pieces of bamboo stuck in the ground to prevent anyone getting close to the camp in a sneak attack. We were always alert, and we needed to be because ambushes were the commonest forms of attack by the enemy.

One morning we heard gunfire an hour after the morning patrol had been sent out. I went out with two jeeps full of armed men but we were too late. All ten men were killed and their weapons taken away. My heart was crushed. I had been about to accompany the patrolling party. At the last moment, I had been persuaded to drop the idea. For days, all I wanted to do was to avenge those men. I felt overwhelmed by guilt and rage. I had not felt that amount of anger over the death of my colleague because that had been an accident. But in the case of the men in the patrol it was so clear they had been waylaid and killed deliberately."

In my days there, I have known many soldiers who have been driven mad by seeing their mates killed beside them. They did terrible things to innocent civilians in turn. War is a dreadful thing *beta*, it blinds you to the horror of what you are doing."

"Neibou's grandfather told him the Indian soldiers tortured many Nagas. Did you ever see anything like that?"

"No. I saw Underground soldiers killed on many occasions. But I never actually saw the tortures of Naga prisoners. But it did happen. You know that interrogations are never nice. In war, sometimes that is the only way to get information on enemy movement.

The feeling of deep vulnerability never left us in Nagaland. We would be traveling by convoy or army jeeps on the open road. So we were always easy targets for the Naga army who used guerilla tactics. In addition, it was difficult to tell who was a soldier and who was not, because the guerillas wore civilian clothes when they came out to the towns. Our men were not used to jungle warfare. Not knowing the language and always isolated in our fortified posts, it was like walking around blindfolded in a mine-field everytime we went out. We felt alienated because we entered Nagaland with the understanding that the Nagas were fellow Indians but the truth was that the Nagas looked completely different and obviously hated our presence there.

Sadly, some of the soldiers posted there suffered serious psychological disorders after their posting. They were always under pressure from the constant tension caused by the atmosphere of alienation. It proved to be too traumatic for them. That is probably one reason for the great numbers of military atrocities committed by the army."

"What do you mean by that Nanna?"

"Raklu, many of those soldiers were boys not much older than the two of you. They found themselves in a situation where they were warring against their own people, after all they had been sent there after being told that the Nagas were Indians. Yet the encounters between the Underground and the army were violent and extremely brutal. The soldiers saw torture of civilians and sometimes participated in it too. It is such a thin dividing line. Some men had nervous breakdowns, those who didn't, turned to brutality. They just let go of their humanity."

Rakesh was listening to all this quietly and then he asked,

"Nanna, you always called the Nagas 'insurgents'. Do you know that Neibou and his people believe that they are a completely different race from Indians? Then it's probably not right to call them insurgents is it?"

"Well, Raklu, I was working for the government and that was the way the government defined them. So I had to use the terms that the government used. We were not there as an occupying force. But we were there to prevent secession by the Nagas from the Indian Union. I don't regret my years in Nagaland. I only wish I could have gone there in peacetime so that I could have befriended the people and done more for them. In war, there is always distrust. It is impossible to do anything constructive in a war environment. I have thought much about it, after I came back.

I greatly admired what I saw of the Nagas. Their culture, their songs, dances, community life and high sense of dignity and self respect. What I liked most was their sense of equality. It is a great thing that the community does so many things together. They also make fine soldiers and guerilla fighters. Even though we were fighting on opposite sides, we could not help admiring their skill in fighting. They moved like shadows, how else could one explain a small band of men holding off large battalions of the Indian army and the Armed Police at the same time? There is something in their culture that produces great tenacity in them as fighters. At least I think so."

"I hope you can travel to Nagaland and meet my grandfather. That would be incredible," said Neibou sincerely.

"It would be a great honour to meet a former warrior," Himmat replied. "Even though he was once my enemy, I bear him no ill-will. We were pawns in a bigger game, that's all. All those men killed. Fathers and sons and husbands. And for what? If the Nagas want their own country, let them have it, that is what I say now. It's none of our business. At least, not to lose so many lives over."

NIRMALA

"**D**on't get too serious, you three," Nirmala called. She was emerging from the kitchen and was now descending on them with cups of tea.

"We won't," Rakesh answered.

"Hey, Raklu, your Nanni was there too, remember? Tell Neibou all about your trip to Nagaland, Nirmala."

"Oh, I don't remember very much because I was so afraid of the sentry."

"Afraid of the sentry? Why Nanni?"

"Well, everytime, your Nanna and I tried to enter the camp, he would aim his rifle at us and ask for the password. I was terrified he would pull the trigger if we forgot the password. You know, as soon as we neared the approach to the camp, I would nag your Nanna to call out the password."

"Ha ha, that she did. She wanted me to call out the password before the sentry could ask me. That would have gotten us into a fine mess since he would not have recognised us in the dark. To tell you the truth, the sentry knew us well but had to do his duty by asking for the password. You never believed me, Nirmala." Himmat said this with a chiding tone in his voice.

"No, I didn't. I had never lived in such an environment before. I was so glad when you were transferred back home."

Nirmala was a practical soul. She had learnt early on in life not to fret over things that were out of her control. So, when her husband was away serving in Nagaland, she had regularly gone to the temple to offer her prayers and sacrifices. With a faith that was as unswerving as it was uncomplicated, she waited for the day of his return. But when she got news of the patrol party ambush, there was nothing that could prevent her from going to him. Once there, she stayed on until his transfer orders allowed him to return to his home state of Madhya Pradesh. Politics never interested her. She could not fathom why people would continue fighting each other for years on end.

"Wouldn't it be so much simpler if the government just gave people what they wanted?" she asked after listening to Himmat explain what the conflict in Nagaland was all about.

"Ah Nirmala," he replied wistfully, "if politicians had your clarity of mind, how much better this country would be run."

"Well," she concluded, not quite sure if Himmat was laughing at her or agreeing with her viewpoint, "I think there are other things that are more important than fighting a war."

She had lived all her life with this simple philosophy. For Himmat, it had been a refuge from the pressures of his profession. In their years together, he was deeply grateful for this level-headedness on her part. When their daughter came home from school, there was always a warm meal waiting. Nirmala gave a certain routine to their family life, not a regimented timetable, but the routine of normality which her husband highly valued. Even now, their life in Bhopal followed very much the same pattern, meals were served punctually, tasty and wholesome meals. She took care to avoid using *ghee* as Himmat's doctor had warned him to keep his cholesterol level down. She found ways of making meals with low-fat recipes without losing out on taste.

When they were visiting their daughter, Nirmala took over the kitchen and Dipti was only too eager to relax and enjoy her mother's cooking. Alok, Dipti's husband worked for a private firm in Faridabad. So he was away during the week. In the old days, he commuted between Faridabad and Haryana on a daily basis. But with traffic multiplying on the highway, it became safer and cheaper for him to live in one of the Faridabad company houses. He came home on weekends. Alok was a quiet man. Even when he was in the house, one barely noticed his presence because he would be sitting in his study reading one of his many books. In his serious moments, Rakesh bore a deep resemblance to his father. That was how he looked right now, his young face somber and thoughtful.

When Nirmala left them alone, Himmat turned to his grandson and asked,

"Something on your mind, Raklu?"

"Oh Nanna, it's difficult to stop thinking. There's so much I have learnt about the Nagas. I have read books on the Naga freedom struggle. There are long lists of Indian army atrocities committed during the 50s. Rapes and tortures of the Naga villagers. Many of them died from torture and starvation. It's horrible to think that our government allowed that to happen."

Himmat looked at his grandson for a long time. Then he said:

"Again, it pains me to tell you that those things did happen. As I said, the army was very brutal with the local people. Not able to fight the enemy, they used fear to control the local population. Some soldiers were so maddened by the deaths of their friends that they picked on civilians and tortured them. The villagers were soft targets. They were unarmed. They were trapped in their villages because they could not survive for long if they fled their village homes. Thinking back on it, I feel that the people who suffered the most were the villagers. They were obliged to give rations to the Underground members when they came asking. Yet they would be punished severely by the Indian army for feeding them.

As a police officer, there were many things I could not speak out against. If I had done that, I would have been seen as a traitor to my government. But now I can speak as an individual. There were many factors involved in that war. The soldiers were very far from their homes. They found themselves fighting an alien culture. You know, the Naga hills are so different from the Indian mainland, one has this feeling that you are in a foreign country. Then there was the language barrier too. It is not surprising that the soldiers were seen as an occupying force. There were the usual linguistic misunderstandings between the soldiers and the local population. The soldiers were nervous and trigger-happy. They had been told that the insurgent groups were experienced and deadly fighters. When you are in fear for your life, you shoot first and ask questions later.

I am rambling on, boys, but there is no way any government can justify what was done to the Nagas in those years. It was not an honourable war and it will stain the reputation of our army forever. Can I tell you two something?" he asked in a low voice.

"Of course," said Neibou.

"What, Nanna?" Rakesh asked.

"Well, when I was about to retire, I actually planned to spend the rest of my life in Nagaland, just setting up something to help the people, a school or something, you know? To help the youngsters to do something meaningful with their lives. I have a bad conscience about what happened there."

"Why didn't you do that then, Nanna?"

"I abandoned it because of your Nanni. Not that she would stop me or anything like that, but it didn't seem fair to her. All our married life, she had taken care of our family home while I travelled from north to south, and east to west on my postings. Many times she could not accompany me. I thought that the least I could do was to make sure we spent the last days of our life together in a peaceful place, leading a quiet life."

"It makes me proud that you had such plans even if you could not fulfill them," said Rakesh.

"Mind you," Himmat replied, wagging his finger at Rakesh, " I have never told her about it, so you shouldn't mention it at all."

"Maybe it is your turn to do something now, you boys," he concluded.

DELHI

Rakesh and Neibou were in the hostel on Sunday night, driven back by Dipti. They were not the only ones in the hostel. More than half of the hostellers had returned. There were the usual noises in the hallway, as the boys boisterously greeted their mates.

Neibou was browsing through the papers when he saw a small item: Northeast girl molested by Holi revellers, denied help by police. He read on. The report said some men had thrown water balloons at a Northeastern girl. When she protested, they molested her. She managed to break free and report the case at the police booth. But the policeman on duty was unwilling to register her case and even shouted at her to shut up. When questioned later by the newspaper reporter, the policeman maintained that he had registered the case immediately and denied having told the woman to shut up.

Feeling a rush of emotions – anger, disgust and frustration Neibou pushed the paper away roughly. Rakesh noticed it and quickly browsed the article. "God, when will they ever stop?" he burst out. "They are animals, there's no other word to describe them. And the policeman – he should be dismissed from his job! Was the case registered at all?"

"After two hours, yes." Neibou replied. "What disgusts me is that we are always alienated and picked on. Today it's a rape, another day it is a stabbing, how are we expected to believe that we are Indians when all this racism goes on? We are served last in a restaurant and cheated by taxis and autos and even rickshaw pullers. Why do they treat us different from other Indians?"

"But Neibou, you are not really Indian!" Rakesh burst out, "I mean, it is so clear to me that you are not."

"I know that. I am Indian on paper because when I fill up a form and they ask for my nationality, I have to write Indian. But many of my Northeastern friends believe that they are ethnically Indians, and when they meet this kind of treatment, they are so traumatised by it. It's deep-rooted racism and its very ugly. The name-calling, the stereo-typing of our girls and the way the police refuse to protect the victim, it just makes me feel very hopeless about the rights we have been promised by the Indian constitution. Becoming a state in India didn't really change anything much. Now we keep encountering maltreatment from the civilian population in place of what we faced earlier at the hands of the army. I doubt things will ever change. In Mumbai, a man attacked and killed a Naga girl. In Pune, five Naga boys were beaten badly by a mob. Yet the government still insists we are all Indians, and tries to ignore the racism."

"You are right about all that. But we can't give in to them, do you see? If we allow ourselves to be depressed by the racists, we will lose the impulse to fight them. If we give up, they will be proved right and they are far from right. We have to help others understand that racism is evil. And if we don't make an effort, the consequence would be reverse racism like what you told me about Indian-hating in Naga circles. That is just as bad. I'm sorry to bring up this comparison but if we are to be honest, giving in to hatred is just as evil and it sets off an ugly cycle."

"Of course," Neibou agreed. "But there is a cruel streak in these people who pick on Northeasterners. They have no ability to accept that we are human beings like any of them."

"No, they are incapable of that. But not everyone in the society is like that. We have to appeal to the good sense of the ones who are more broad-minded and compassionate. Like the women's groups and the people who believe in them. Human Rights groups here in the city are fighting this sort of oppression too, aren't they? We have to find human solutions to all these problems that have been engendered by political conflicts. After all, it's the people who matter and not some stupid political theory."

Neibou brooded all morning over the report. The two of them drafted off a protest letter to the National Human Rights Commission, but Neibou was not entirely satisfied with the draft and tore it up. Then they wrote instead to the National Commission for Women and posted it off in the afternoon.

OUT ON THE PORCH
2007

Neituo shuffled his way into the porch and sat down beside Mose. The latter nodded absently.

"Well, how was it?" Neituo asked.

"How was what?"

"The action today, Neilhounuo tells me you were in the thick of the shooting at the market."

"She should start her own radio station, that woman," Mose muttered.

"You better tell me all then," said Neituo with his old grin back in place.

It had been a long time since Mose had seen that. Neituo, widowed for three years now, had remained downcrest for a long time after Thejaviü's sudden death. Mose was pleased that he could see a bit of the old Neituo re-emerging in the last few weeks.

"Well?" Neituo prodded.

"Oh that? They were two young men, boys really, not much older than Neibou. No one noticed them at first, or maybe people thought they were playing the fool. They were scuffling for a bit before one pulled out a gun and the other tried to run. He was shot in the back. It took some seconds before anyone realised what had happened. The killer came in my direction and tried to push me out of his way," Mose finished.

"Oh, where were you?"

"I was standing close by, a bit shocked but not terrified. I remember thinking, I want to get a good look at his face. He swung the pistol round and pushed me and shouted, 'Get out of the way, old man!' Then he ran off toward the Dak Lane street. No one tried to stop him. Everyone was too frightened."

"No police around?"

"No, not until twenty minutes after the killing."

"Well, you should know that these people wouldn't hesitate to shoot you if you were in their way."

"Yes, I was keenly aware of that, but what's to be done, Neituo? In a way, I feel responsible since we were once among the first group who started to fight for independence. Now, it is so far from what it originally was."

"Yes, we have two wars now. The one with the Indian government and the other is the one among our own people. When we are so divided, we don't have much hope for the future."

"No, we don't," Mose agreed. "It looks very bleak, doesn't it? I wonder if we will annihilate ourselves completely with all this killing."

"And you're unusually dark tonight," Neituo commented.

"Hard not to be, after seeing what I did," said Mose.

"It was factional members today, wasn't it?" Neituo asked and continued without waiting for an answer. "Of course it was another factional killing. All that big noise about peace talks between India and the NSCN(IM) and no one bothers about the killings here. The only way it's going to work is by starting peace talks between the factions first. Get them to stop killing each other and then we can talk about terms of peace with India. But not before we have stopped killing each other."

Mose said nothing so Neituo continued after a pause, "It's crazy to see what has been spawned out of a single-minded fight for freedom. If a complete stranger came here, an outsider, and asked, 'What is the problem with you Nagas? What do you really want?' I would say to him, 'All we want is peace, unbelievable as that might seem. We have the strangest of stories here and it is this: First, we were fighting Indian occupation from 1947 and doing a good job of it until factionalism entered in 1975. Then we were plagued by infighting that made everyone think we were quite mad because the factionalism made Nagas kill their fellow Nagas. Then the Indian government used the lure of money to destroy our integrity and impose Indian citizenship on us. Now we have all sorts of complications. Naga children are being taught they are Indians but when they go to the Indian cities they are completely alienated by the Indian population. Another problem is home-grown state terrorism. We have seen the growth of the Indian Reserve Battalions and their fearfully abusive conduct, and now we have almost come full circle because people today fear the Indian army less than they fear their own men! As for the Indian army, they don't have it so good either. I hear some of the Indian soldiers of yesterday are victims of extreme angst, traumatised by what they had experienced in the Naga Hills. Who would think it would come to that? Stranger, it may seem absurd to you but all we really want is peace. That and our land.'"

Neilhounuo's voice disrupted them.

"You two better not stay up late, what with the killing in town. Don't keep Neituo long, Mose."

It was a command, not a request.

"Just ten more minutes Neilhounuo, we are discussing Neituo's marriage prospects," Mose shouted back and threw a look at Neituo.

"Yes, that's right," shouted Neituo. "We just found out that there are some 35-year-old divorcees very interested in 70-year-old war hero widowers."

"You can't fool me with that anymore," Neilhounuo shouted back.

The two friends exchanged looks.

"She is right," said Neituo getting up out of his chair. "It is late, I can come by tomorrow."

"Sorry about that, the old woman's gotten so crotchety these days. I can't wait for Neibou to come back and put her in a good mood."

"Oh, when is he due?" Neituo asked.

"Four days from now, I think that's what Sabunuo said."

"Wonderful, we need some young blood around here. We're too old even to keep shop."

The two said goodnight and Mose sat outside for some time more.

Neituo shuffled his way down the steps and went home. Neituo had never fully recovered from the injury to his left leg. It had worsened over the years. It left him with a permanent shuffling, which slowed him down comparatively. Always positive, he had commented,

"Makes me look more interesting to the women. Makes them wonder what old war wound it was that's left me disabled. I can always start up a conversation with this new stylish walk of mine."

Mose watched him go. How old they both were now. He was seventy, Neituo seventy-one. It had been a long lifetime and much of it shadowed by war.

THE VISIT

"**G**randfather!" called out a young voice. Mose turned round to see two tall young men at his door.

"How did you steal up without me noticing?" he asked as he warmly greeted his grandson. Next he held out his hand to the newcomer, and welcomed Rakesh into his household.

The boys explained that they had arrived late the night before. But they had slept in and woken late, and now they were ready for the meal Mose had invited them to.

Mose spoke to Rakesh in English and broken Hindi, surprising Neibou a bit.

"I didn't know you could speak Hindi, Grandfather," he remarked.

"Ah...still plenty you don't know about me," Mose smiled.

"What are you doing standing here? Come in, come in," said Neilhounuo to the men. She led the way into the house and wiped away a fine layer of dust on the chairs.

"*Npezie*," Rakesh offered.

"*Hou!*" said Neilhounuo with a pleased smile and she patted him on the arm.

Neilhounuo was a gracious hostess. She always was. Her inability to speak Hindi did not deter her from addressing Rakesh in Tenyidie and he nodded his head politely and said, 'O, *npezie*,' several times. The phrase Neibou had taught him meant 'yes, thank you.' Of course, Rakesh did not understand a word of what Neilhounuo was saying but he smiled his affable smile and said 'O' to most of what she said, including her query on what his name was. The others laughed and Rakesh looked confused. "You just answered yes to the question, 'What is your name?'" Neibou laughingly explained. Neilhounuo soothed Rakesh, "It's not your fault, how were you to know?" which Rakesh didn't understand either.

They proceeded to teach Rakesh how to respond in Tenyidie to simple questions. The lunch turned out to be quite a humourous experiment what with the language teaching that was going on simultaneously. Neibou noticed that his Grandmother had covered the table with her best tablecloth. She used it only on rare occasions. He was touched to see that. He also noticed that she was using new plates and cups.

"Very nice plates, Grandmother," he said loudly to show her he appreciated her efforts at hosting. She blushed a bit and said,

"Oh, you mean those? I bought them from a woman who brings Burmese goods around here every month. They are sturdy plates," she said with an emphasis on the long lasting quality of the plates.

"They look pretty too," Neibou observed.

"Ah, that too," she admitted almost reluctantly. That was typical of Grandmother, Neibou thought. She would not waste her money on something that could not be put to some good use. Neibou helped her to set the table while Mose continued to tell Rakesh about his life in the Underground. Soon, food was served and two very hungry young men did justice to the cooking.

"Wonderful food, Grandmother," said Neibou sincerely, "You are such a good cook." Rakesh turned to her too and said,

"*Npezie ho*." Rakesh's awkward pronounciation made everybody laugh again. He stressed in the wrong places and his intonation was a little off-key. Quite understandably, because Tenyidie was an extremely tonal language where a word changed completely in meaning depending on the tone.

"It's not easy, my child, but you have learnt the best words," Neilhounuo spoke encouragingly to him. Neibou translated for her.

By the time dinner was over, everyone was visibly relaxed. Spontaneous laughter could be heard at Rakesh's mistakes and Mose's rough Hindi.

"Well, my Hindi is rusty now," Mose admitted, "but when we were in the Underground, we learned Hindi to be able to decipher what the soldiers were saying to each other. I can still learn more if I get enough practice."

Neilhounuo smiled at this and said,

"Maybe it would help if you watched some Hindi movies." They laughed at the idea of Mose watching Hindi movies on television or at a video hall in town.

Mose spoke a halting Hindi which sounded odd in his highly accentuated voice but Rakesh patiently listened to him. Eventually, they grew used to each other's manner of speaking. Through a few phrases and gestures they managed to reach an effective method of communication. Mose turned to Neilhounuo to tell her things about Rakesh's life. Rakesh looked at Neibou and said,

"Man, your grandparents are great. And your Grandad is so smart." Neibou smiled back at him and replied,

"I am very proud of them both, you know that."

"You have every reason to be."

Neibou sat on in a corner while his grandfather and Rakesh continued their conversation. He was thinking of his days as a child in this very room. It felt very long ago.

"Neibou," his grandmother called out, "shall I make you some red tea?"

"Sure, Grandmother, I am a grown man now, I can drink red tea." Funny that it was only amongst Nagas that they called it red tea. In all other places it was called black tea. She poured out a medium sized mug for him. Neibou answered questions on how their studies were going. By the time they finished, Neibou realised that it was later than usual for his grandparents, who kept early hours. Rising to his feet he said to Rakesh,

"We had better be going, Rocky, because it is now an hour past their bedtime." Rakesh jumped to his feet, and took leave of the old couple. "*Npezie ho, ho,*" he said, evoking as much laughter as he had the first time he said it. Promising to return, the two young men walked down the darkened path.

All of the next week the two friends travelled to the villages surrounding Kohima. At the end of the week, they reported on their travels to Mose and Neilhounuo to their great entertainment.

ON THE TRAIN

"This really was a fun trip," said Rakesh to Neibou on the train. "Let's do it again soon."

"Oh definitely," replied Neibou. "My grandparents liked you very much, as did my parents."

"Well I liked them a lot, and I can't wait to tell my family about them." They sat facing each other and talking excitedly about all they had seen and done in Kohima. They were so full of good memories that neither of them felt the tediousness of the long journey back.

Their train had already crossed Guwahati. The rich lands of lower Assam stretched out before them. Rice fields that were yellow and ready to be harvested. They could see workers in some of the fields reaping the ripe stalks. The train ride through this part of the country was never boring. After the rice fields, they passed little hamlets where houses with neat mud walls stood. People were going about their evening works. There were fishermen returning home with the day's catch. Their long nets swayed in the breeze as they walked homeward. Some children ran towards them from the houses. The bamboo groves and clumps of coconut trees were restful to look upon. When the sun set, they watched the scarlet skies slowly grow dim until the sun was a small red ball in the grey sky.

They were both lost in their own thoughts, each remembering the trip and all the things they had seen. Neibou was happy at how well the trip had gone, though a year and a half had gone by before they could make the trip. He was especially pleased that Rakesh had liked his mother's cooking. It had been good to go home and let Rakesh get to know his family. All of it had brought them closer. It was strange. He had never expected to become such good friends with an Indian boy. The suspicion that most Nagas felt towards Indians had intensified when he was being ragged at college. That had been a lonely period of his life when he had even contemplated giving up everything and returning back home. In the college next to theirs, some Naga boys had been beaten by the locals for eating meat. All these things had been very depressing when it happened. Rakesh had given him, in a way, the determination he needed to stick to his goal. He looked across at his friend.

Rakesh had a faraway look in his eyes. All the place-names that grandfather Himmat used to mention had never really meant anything to him before. Mokokchung, Dimapur, Kohima, Jakhama. He recalled his grandfather talking of these places. When his grandfather spoke of them, he imbued them with a certain mysterious atmosphere which Rakesh was closer to understanding now. In many ways, Nagaland was so different from the rest of India. He had heard Hindi songs being played from the odd corner-shop in Dimapur and Kohima. But on the whole, to be in Naga towns and villages, seemed like being in another country altogether.

Rakesh struggled to define what he had seen in the past ten days. It was no Shangrila, though it had been difficult enough to reach. In some places, it seemed to him that time had come to a standstill and the people lived on, trapped in another century. He had felt that when he was in Mose's house. The old-world charm and hospitality was something he had not seen in Delhi. Life was slower in Kohima. But sadder too, immensely sad. Kohima was steeped in grief. People smiled and greeted him warmly, but there was always some terrible tragedy behind their smiles. Some member of the family killed in the war years with India or even now, young male relatives shot in factional encounters. It was as though all families carried unhealed wounds from the conflict in some way or the other. There was a present sense of fear that permeated normal life and everything would come to a standstill at the sound of a single gunshot. Still, life went on and people recovered from the sudden interruptions and went on living their lives until it was interrupted again.

On the last day of their stay, they had heard a terrible thing. A man in his forties, a neighbour of Neibou's, had been abducted. They didn't hear anything more about him before they left. But Neibou said that he would most likely be killed. The incident cast a pall over them all and everyone fell silent for a long time.

Rakesh had not noticed the sadness immediately. It struck him only after some days that life was far from idyllic in Kohima. The way people spoke carefully, measuring their words if they were talking about the conflict, the way they wanted to appear neutral and not part of it, not siding any one group. Amongst younger people there was a tendency to joke irreverently about the 'National Workers' as the cadres were called. But the elders were tight-lipped when anyone mentioned them. Even Mose's face had hardened when Rakesh had asked him about it. 'It is no longer an honourable thing that they are doing, my son,' he had said curtly.

So these were the Nagas, he thought. The people the Indian army had feared and called "vile terrorists." These smiling-faced farmers and shopkeepers. So very different from what he had expected. He could see why grandfather Himmat had wanted to settle there.

A FATAL ACCIDENT

Mose was alone at home. It was a month after the boys had left for Delhi. The day was sunny so he took his hoe and went to work a bit in the back yard. He would plant the tree-tomato behind the house. It was good for it to get morning sun. It was so peaceful outside and he could hear the cries of migratory birds. How his mother had liked that sound. She would often stop working and stand still and listen to the birds. Mose began to dig the hole for the tree-tomato.

Suddenly, he heard a great commotion. Shouting, angry voices and a thin, frightened voice calling out, "Baba, Baba!" Mose recognised it as Jitu's voice, the Bihari boy who ran a *paan* shop on the corner. Mose didn't know who the others were. Without hesitating, he rushed down the path, waving his walking stick and shouting, "Who is it? Hey, stop fighting!" as he tried to reach the shop.

There were two men there. Mose saw the Bihari shopkeeper lying on the ground, being kicked and beaten by the strangers. They were shouting, "You're lying, you have more money than that!" The men continued to beat the boy, aiming for his head and stomach.

"Leave him alone, you thugs!" Mose shouted, coming forward with his cane raised high. One of the men quickly turned and shot twice at the approaching figure. Mose crumpled to the ground, a bullet in his throat and another in his chest. The men ran off when they saw the old man fall down, bleeding profusely. The Bihari boy realised what had happened and crawled to his side, screaming loudly, "Baba, Baba!"

Mose died instantly. The Bihari boy cradled Mose's head on his lap and called out for help. Some children came running. Quickly they were sent to fetch Sabunuo and Vilalhou. The two came immediately. Someone else was sent to fetch Neilhounuo from the village where she had gone to visit a relative.

The small group silently carried Mose's body back to the house. There was a pool of blood on the path from the shop to Mose's house. They managed to wash it away before Neilhounuo arrived. The whole colony was shocked. The old couple had led a peaceful existence and no one could have imagined that Mose would die in such a violent manner.

When she reached the road, Neilhounuo ran into the house in a frenzy.

"Mose, Mose, somebody tell me it is not true!" she shouted as she clutched at her husband's motionless body. "*Ayalie* Mose, not this way, how can I bear this?" she wept aloud. She began to shake uncontrollably and the others took her to her room to rest, but she was distraught with grief.

Neituo was the next person to arrive. Looking more stooped than usual, he cried out, "Mose! Am I not your best

friend? How can you go without saying goodbye to me?"
He sat by the body all throughout the day and refused to
leave. "We only have today, bear with me," he pleaded with
his niece who tried to persuade him to come out and rest
a bit. Sabunuo was numb with grief too, but she made an
attempt to compose herself to look after the arrangements
for the burial.

Mose was given a big funeral. The number of mourners
surprised Sabunuo and Vilalhou. They saw how well loved
Mose was in the community. Several speeches were made
by former companions in the Underground, by relatives and
finally, by the Pastor of his church. The front yard was filled
with people and the neighbours let them use their yard to
accomodate the mourners.

Neibou had taken the first flight back to Dimapur when
he heard the news. The unbelievable sadness that he had felt
when he was first told was quickly supplanted by cold anger.
Not just at the killer, but at the whole Naga situation that had
been the setting for the killing of his grandfather. He fully
understood now why the cycle of vengeance killing continued
to be perpetrated when a factional member was killed. Peace
loving as he was, the news of his grandfather's shooting made
him feel murderous. He wanted to make those responsible
suffer in some way.

Yet in the midst of all that he managed to whisper, 'Thank
God it wasn't a premeditated murder.' That would have been
even harder to deal with.

Nevertheless, the killers could not be exonerated lightly.
They had acted in a very irresponsible manner. They had not
meant to kill him or even hit him, they had sent word. The shots
were fired to frighten him off, they claimed. Responding to

questions from his family through the underground network, they said they had no idea of his identity. The leaders of the faction involved asked to meet the family members, saying they wanted to give them some money as compensation. But no one from the family wanted to meet them. The idea of taking compensation money from the faction was loathsome to Mose's family members.

Once he was in Kohima, Neibou sent them a message that was both harsh and honest. He described the caring and dedicated man his grandfather had been, how he had devoted his best years to the Naga cause, and in old age, had endeavoured to teach the values of their culture to his grandchildren. He ended with the appeal to the factional leaders to teach their members about the worth of each human life and how irreplaceable it was when taken away. They did hear back from certain sources that the faction deeply regretted the incident.

Neituo was unable to accept Mose's death. He would go to the grave and look at it uncomprehendingly and then return home, mumbling to himself in resignation: "Ah my friend, we lived by the sword, so we have died by the sword."

The Bihari paan seller was distraught at the tragic turn of events. "*Baba, Baba,*" he would wail, sitting by Mose's grave every morning for long periods. To any passer-by he would say, "*Baba ami karna morise, aya Baba morise.*" Family members tried explaining to him that it was an accident. But he kept blaming himself for the killing. Every morning, he came to the grave and wept over it and then returned to his shop. After a week, his sister and brother came to him. They

Baba ami karna morise: Father died because of me

tearfully thanked Neibou's family. "If not for Baba, our brother would surely have died that day," they said over and over again. His family members wanted to take him back to Bihar with them. But he refused. "How can I leave *Amma* now?" he asked. He was referring to Neilhounuo. So the young man stayed on in Kohima, performing a strange penance of his own by taking care of Mose's grave and bringing gifts of food to Neilhounuo.

AFTERWARDS

Neilhounuo was shattered by the tragedy. It was the first time Sabunuo saw her hard-faced mother crumple. From the day of the shooting she began to look weak and old and frail. Before her daughter's very eyes, she aged. It surprised Sabunuo and at first she didn't know how to cope with this new mother. Gradually their roles became reversed and Sabunuo found herself becoming care-giver for the woman who had always provided care for her, well into the years of her married life.

Neibou was the one who noticed that his grandmother's hair had turned fully white almost overnight. Gently he smoothed down the strands that had slipped out of her chignon. "We are still here, Grandmother," he said soothingly. She looked up at him with eyes gone old and helpless. That look constricted his heart and he had to fight hard not to cry. Is this what death does? he thought.

There was a lot to do after the funeral. Going through his grandfather's papers and sorting them out. Sabunuo had carefully packed all of Mose's clothes into a big suitcase. When her mother was able to, they would sit together and sort out what to give away and what to keep. Neibou stayed two days more, doing what he could to help his mother.

"You will probably find something that interests you there. Seeing that you were the closest to him, I'm sure your grandfather would have liked you to look after his papers." So Neibou went about his job with all seriousness. He felt honoured.

Neibou was fascinated by what he found. Letters and Applications written to the British Parliament from 1929, asking for the Naga Hills to be returned to a sovereign status when the British gave up their South Asian empire. There were letters addressed to various members of the House of Lords by name, one to a Lord Simon and one to Sir Winston Churchill. There was a document on the nine-point agreement with Sir Akbar Hydari at Shillong. The Hydari agreement offered protection to Naga customary practices for a ten-year period after which the terms would be reviewed. There were at least two letters to the Secretary General, UN. Written in impeccable English, the letters stated clearly the right of the Nagas to be a free people when Indian and Burmese independence was secured. Neibou found a file to put the letters into. They were so old they seemed to be falling apart.

In the same shelf he found a journal. Curiously he opened it and went through the yellowed pages. Neibou recalled that his grandfather liked to jot down things and hang them on bits of paper above his bed. The old leather-bound diary bore Mose's name. In it were recorded dates and events. Neibou's date of birth. Above that, lined in red ink was Sabounuo's birthday. Why was it underlined in red ink? Another date that was thus underlined was March 25, 1963 and the words, patrolling party next to it. Could this have been the attack on the patrolling party Himmat had told them about?

The dates written in red ink were obviously all important events. One was the Plebiscite day, 16 May, 1951. Another was the 14 August 1947, the Naga Independence day and the Naga Republic day. All those dates were familiar to Neibou. But he wondered about the other dates in red ink. Apart from birthdays of their family members, what were the other important dates in his grandfather's life? Who would know? Would his grandmother be able to tell him?

Years ago, the Indian army, ransacking a gaonbura's house in Phekerükrie village, had found letters bearing Phizo's signature. The gaonbura survived the beating but was maimed for life. Neibou felt the irony of it so many years later. It was obvious that his grandfather had hidden the documents in various places before feeling secure enough to keep them below his bed along with other documents such as the *patta* papers to his house and land. On one of the papers, a bit of red soil betrayed where it had lain for many months.

Neibou mused over that. Mose's generation was obssessed about dates. They secretly celebrated Naga independence day every 14th August. At these celebrations, an elder would get up to retell how the Naga delegation that met Mahatma Gandhi had decided to declare Naga independence on the day before Indian independence day. That made them a nation older to India by a day, he would always add. The elder would carefully explain that Gandhiji had expressly told them that they had every right to declare their independence. Groups furtively met on this day and held celebrations. At the Peace

Patta: land deed

Camps in Kohima and Chedema, the celebrations went on publicly, but smaller groups were forced to be secretive about their celebrations because it was an outlawed activity.

Browsing through the documents, Neibou suddenly remembered something he had read. A psychoanalyst had stated that some races were preoccupied with documenting and chronicling because it satisfied a deep need for legitimacy. Diaries, journals and biographic writing were all quoted as examples of this search for legitimising oneself. The races most interested in documenting were those emerging from oral cultures. Certificates were of great value to them. Birth certificates, land pattas, applications, letters, these were all filed to be duly presented if any doubt as to the legitimacy of their claims arose.

After some time, Neibou dusted off the journal and closed it. Not today. Some other time he would ask his grandmother about it. What should he do with Grandfather's papers? Both his mother and grandmother suggested that he take it home with him. He threw most of the other papers away. Old magazines and newspapers from the 1960s. Paper cuttings from *The Statesman*, a long article about the abnormal expenses of the army in Nagaland. One of the clippings was a report about an Indian Air force plane shot down over Nagaland. The picture showed the crew being released by the Naga Underground. It was a blurry photograph of four men. Neibou retrieved these cuttings intending to go through them when he had more time.

"Come and eat something," his mother called. Neibou set the box aside carefully and joined them in the kitchen. His grandmother sat at the table, pecking at her food.

"Mother, you will fall sick if you don't eat properly,"

Sabunuo nagged. Neilhounuo looked at her daughter and said,

"I have no appetite."

"Please try," her daughter urged. She threw a look at her son. "Grandmother, please do eat for our sakes," Neibou implored her. She looked at him without saying anything. Neibou was a little worried that he might have displeased her. But in the next moment she said slowly,

"All right, child," she said and began to eat. She even managed a weak smile.

PUSHING HISTORY OUT

At Delhi's Indira Gandhi airport, Rakesh was waiting when Neibou's flight landed. None of them said very much. Later, at Rakesh's house, Neibou filled them in on the details of the killing and the funeral. The big funeral had shown the affection for Mose in his neighbourhood and amongst his clansmen. For Neibou, there was some healing in being able to talk about it. The three of them were seated in Dipti's living room, talking about Mose's murder.

"Will they serve a prison term?" Dipti asked. Neibou shook his head. That was not likely.

"That is preposterous, even if they claim it was an accident, they have to serve a term of some sort. One cannot be so dismissive of the loss of a human life."

Neibou had nothing to say to that. His grandfather was not the first to die in a shooting accident. Nor would he be the last. The police would intervene and try to get the guilty to negotiate with the family. But beyond that, they would go for settlement of the case between the two parties and not press charges directly. Some of the impotent rage he had felt when he first heard the news returned. Rakesh, ever sensitive to his friend's moods, noticed it.

"A lot of things would have to happen before we can secure justice in Nagaland," said Rakesh. He looked at his mother as he said this.

"Such as?" Dipti asked.

"Well, for one, these thugs would have to be made to understand what they did was wrong. But they are deeply brutalised. That is the term Nanna was using. They need help to be debrutalised."

"How is that going to happen?" Dipti asked, "Who can make that happen?"

"I don't know, Mom," Rakesh answered. "Imprisoning them will only harden them further. These are the sort of men who will need a life-changing experience in order to turn them around. For some, it might even be too late."

"Something of a spiritual nature you mean? A conversion experience, maybe?"

"Well, yes, why not? Something extraordinary that takes away the self-destructiveness and makes them want to be better persons."

"But they do have all of that in Christianity don't they? And they are Christians, aren't they?"

There was a soft knock at the door. It was the maid was bringing in cups of tea which they gratefully took. Between sips, Neibou began to explain,

"You know, we do call ourselves a Christian state, but many people don't realise that Christianity is a lifestyle and not just a religion," he paused a second. "The Christianity we have today has been perverted, because people don't live Christ-like lives. They think that as long as they are church-going, they are okay. The factions have even used the slogan, 'Nagaland for

Christ' and killed drug addicts and drug pushers. As if that is what God would have wanted."

"No, no, that is all wrong," Dipti agreed.

"I've often despaired over my people and the situation at home," Neibou continued. "When you have grown up in it, it's easy to lose faith early on, and Grandfather's death sort of seemed to confirm it all. But if I give up, what is left for me? Or all the others? Now that I am away from it, I understand things more clearly. I have an overview now, in a way."

"That's a very lucid thought," said Dipti encouragingly, "do go on."

"Well, for one, the distance helps me to think without emotional attachment. I don't want to wallow in self-pity. Rather, I want to do something to help debrutalise those who are trapped in the conflict, like the cadres for example. Some practical training that they can use to rebuild their lives. The practical training may not be so difficult, but getting the violence out of them will be much more challenging."

"I can see that," said Dipti. "It's about learning to let go of the past. I shouldn't really say so much as I have never experienced the hurt and pain these people have. But I know that if they could deconstruct history, they could create their own solutions."

"Hmm...deconstruct history? As in detaching oneself? Or?" Neibou leaned forward.

Rakesh, who had been sitting quietly all this while, listening to his mother and his friend, burst in,

"Mom, it's very different for the Nagas. They are very proud of their warrior ancestry. They wouldn't agree with doing away with their history."

There was an awkward silence at this. Dipti drank the last of her tea and began again,

"I'm just trying to say, in some situations, history kills solutions. So one has to simply push it out. Adapt it. Focus on the present moment, and on the people who are alive today, not those who are dead and gone. Times have changed. People need to stop going on about who did what to who. There is no future in that."

"I completely agree. We have to learn to let the past remain where it is. The trouble with us Nagas is that we have allowed the conflict to define us for too long. It has overtaken our lives so much that we have been colonised by it and its demands on us. But we do not have to let it continue to define us and limit us. It only otherises us again and again. In this day and age it has simply made our lives unnecessarily complicated. We are still allowing ourselves to be bound by cultural dictates and the culture of the conflict itself. I saw that for myself after my grandfather's killing. Immediately after the funeral we had a big problem at home. My clansmen were so upset over Grandfather's death that they began to plot to find the two men and kill them. We had to ask our village council to intervene."

"Of course, they would feel that way," said Dipti. "It's a miracle you have taken it so well. At your age, and having been so close to your grandfather, it would come as no surprise if you had tried to take the law into your own hands."

"Oh I wanted to, when the news first sank in, I felt more rage than sorrow. I thought that if I could avenge him, it would somewhat assuage my loss. It would have been a manly thing to just take a gun and shoot somebody in revenge."

"What stopped you?"

"My grandfather did. Not that he revealed anything from

beyond the grave, but it was simply the things he had taught me. I remembered how he used to say that we fight wars in order to protect ourselves, not to force our will on others. The man who takes up the gun, must be sure he does it for the right reasons. That reason, he said, should be love, not hate."

"Wisdom from a man who was speaking from experience, having lived the life he led. And that helped you?"

"I put my trust in my grandfather's teachings. I realised if I did anything violent, my action would actually hurt Grandfather, instead of honouring him. It hasn't been easy. But now I have peace in the decision. How would it help if we had killed his killers? It wouldn't bring Grandfather back to life, and there would only be more dead to avenge."

"I'm proud of you, Neibou. It may be seen as the manly thing in many cultures to take revenge. But what you have chosen is a much harder thing. How is your grandmother coping?"

"It's a great struggle for her, the worst in her life."

The phone rang. The shrill sound broke into their conversation and Rakesh jumped to get it. "Nanna! How are you? Yes, we are all well. Yes, he's here with us, do you want to speak to him?"

Rakesh handed the phone to Neibou. It was a long conversation. When he replaced the receiver, Neibou had tears in his eyes.

"Are you all right?" Rakesh asked anxiously.

"I'll be fine. Himmat was telling me that he had planned to visit Kohima ever since he met me. He had had a dream of meeting my grandfather. But I guess that wasn't on the cards for them. How great it would have been if they could have met."

"Yes, they would have had so much to talk about."

BITTER WORMWOOD

At Dimapur airport, the plane landed with a loud bump. Then it skidded and came to a sudden halt. Passengers let out involuntary cries of alarm. However, the pilot managed to steady the airplane and veer away from the undergrowth at the edge of the airfield. Sighs of relief went up as the sound system crackled into life. Neibou climbed off the plane gingerly. So much had happened in these past months. He felt as though he would need a long time to digest it all. Rakesh had accompanied him on this trip. They had finished their final exams so they were simply waiting for the results.

They took a taxi to Kohima, persuading the driver to take them all the way home for an extra fifty rupees. There was a bit of haggling over the price, but when the taxi driver was convinced that it was on the main highway, he finally agreed.

"Neibou!" his mother cried out at their approach. She welcomed them both heartily. The house was full of people, which was usual for that time of day. Sabunuo's weavers were still at work and two of them were busy selecting yarn, so there were lengths of yarn spread out on the table as the two women put together different shades to see if they matched. They were both new workers. When Sabunuo introduced them to her son and his friend, they expressed surprise that she had such a grown son.

After some time, the three of them were left alone.

"How's Grandmother?"

"She is better than expected. She was quite sick in the week you left. We didn't tell you as we didn't want to worry you. Since then, she has not been sick again. She is eating well now. You can go by and meet her later."

"We'll do that, Mother."

"Now you must eat something," said his mother as she bustled off to serve them food.

They both sat in the kitchen, tired from the long journey. There was a small crack in the wall which his father had not found the time to mend. Neibou got up to examine it. The plaster had cracked when it was being painted.

"Hmm, I could repair that," he said to no one in particular. His mother heard him.

"Shoddy carpentry," she explained. "That is what happens when everyone is in a hurry. You get bad workmanship." She placed plates of steaming rice before them. In small china bowls, she served them meat and greens and tathu, red chillies crushed into roasted tomatoes and dried fish. Neibou's mouth watered.

"Nothing like home food. I forgot how much I have missed it."

"Eat well, you have a long holiday this time, don't you?"

"That's right, Mother. Well, we have finished with College now. So the next step is either job-hunting or further studies."

Rakesh thanked her for the meal when they were done.

"Don't you want to rest a bit?" she asked when they got up to go.

"We want to visit Grandmother before it gets too late for her," explained Neibou.

"Oh yes, do that."

Neilhounuo was very happy to see the two boys.

"Hmm...I know this one," she said, pointing her finger at Rakesh.

"But who is this stranger?" she squinted at Neibou.

"I'm sorry I couldn't get back earlier, Grandmother," Neibou explained. "We were having our final exams."

Neilhounuo wanted to feed them but they insisted that they were not hungry at all. She led them out to the backyard where Mose's grave was. Someone had smoothed the red earth on the grave. "How nice the grave looks. Have you been doing that, Grandmother?"

"No, it was that sweet *deshwali* boy, *t*he paan seller. His name is Jitender, but we all call him Jitu. He comes every Thursday to do that. In the beginning he would come with flowers. The yellow marigolds, you know the ones I mean. The poor boy must have collected all that he could find from the neihgbourhood. He would put them in a bottle with water and place it on the grave, crying, 'Baba, aya, Baba' all the time. Now he doesn't cry as much. Just comes to do the grave. But sometimes he stands there a long time and cries. I comfort him when he does that. It's a funny situation. I'm so touched that someone who is not even a family member

Deshwali: literally son of the soil in Hindi, but used by Nagas to refer to labourers from Bihar

would be so affected by your grandfather's death. This boy thinks of your grandfather as his saviour."

"That's nice, Grandmother. But in a way, if it hadn't been for him, Grandfather would still be alive today, wouldn't he?"

"I don't think so, Neibou. We believe everyone has a special time allotted to all of us. If it had not been in that manner, your grandfather would have died in some other way that day. It was his time."

"Is that what you believe, Grandmother?"

"I do. I found peace when I realised that the things said by our people through the years are true. Your grandfather was not a violent man, you know that. But he lived much of his life using the gun. He had to. So he has died by the gun."

Neibou looked up at her eagerly as she said that.

"Grandmother, in our culture we are supposed to take revenge on those who kill our loved ones. Have I have failed in my duty because I did not do anything? I mean, since I didn't do anything to avenge him, wouldn't others think that I didn't love Grandfather?"

Neilhounuo looked at him for some moments and then spoke carefully,

"That is the old culture, my child. We cannot live like that anymore. It will destroy us. Before our people came to Jisu, we did that. But now, we are to take our burdens to Jisu and leave it with him. Some men take it upon themselves to minister judgement. When they do that, nothing good can come of it. Leave it with Jisu, I say. Mark my words, child, I have seen it in my own lifetime. Several times."

She walked back towards the house, a small, stooped figure.

The two friends remained outside by the grave.

"I still struggle with the part where the pastor said we should forgive and forget," said Neibou. "I can't agree with that. I can't forget, even if I am able to forgive. You know he said that at the funeral," he confided to his friend.

"Did he say that? Do you have to forget?" Rakesh asked in some surprise. "You can choose to forget the anger and the hurt. But how can it be possible to forget how your grandfather died? If you are not able to forgive, it's all right, give it time. At least that is how I see it."

"I have forgiven.." Neibou replied, "not so much the men.. but the act itself. I always need to stop and remind myself of that so I don't get eaten up by the bitterness. I'd be of no use to anyone if I let this destroy me," said Neibou.

"That's very well said. Your grandfather would want you to come out of it a bigger person, wouldn't he?" Rakesh asked.

"He would. Yet, it's such darkness sometimes. I don't know how to say this properly. When I cling to my decision of forgiveness, I feel as though I'm flinging myself into that darkness again. It's not a one-time act. It is an ongoing thing. I have to continue forgiving, even when I least feel like it. Maybe that is not the right word for what I choose to do. Maybe it is not forgiving that I do, but something else...like.. like..choosing to survive, oh you know what I mean," Neibou ended with a faltering voice.

"Forgiveness is a big, big word," Rakesh agreed. "We have to reach it gradually. It is the destination, not the doorway."

"Is that something from Hindu philosophy?" Neibou asked curiously.

"Nope," his friend smiled, "I just came upon it a few seconds ago."

"That's not bad," said Neibou as he bent to pluck a leaf from a plant by the grave.

"What's that?" Rakesh asked.

"Bitter wormwood," Neibou explained. "It's a herb we use for cuts and insect bites. When I was young, Grandfather would pluck that and put it behind my ear on our way to the forest. 'That will keep the bad spirits away from you, the leaf will make sure they don't get at you,' he would say."

"Bitter wormwood," said Rakesh wonderingly, "what a ominous name for a plant, yet kind of an interesting metaphor. I guess the Nagas of today have forgotten to use it."

"I guess so," said Neibou. "Maybe we should start using it again. We sure could do with some of that old magic now."

The two turned from the grave and walked towards the house. At the entrance, Neibou paused and looked back. The first of the evening's cicadas began their serenade. Neibou held the leaf to his face and inhaled deeply. Images rushed through his mind.

He smiled a little to himself and looked at the oddly-shaped leaf in his hand. Shrugging slightly, he tucked it behind his ear and turned. The wind stung him through his thin shirt. The warmth of the sun had gone with the fading light. He shuddered a little, and quickly walked into the lighted doorway.

Some Important Dates of Naga Political History

1832–1947: British Occupation of the Naga Hills.

1918: Naga Club formed, an organization of Nagas initiated for political awareness.

1929: Simon Commission. The Naga Club submits a memorandum to the Simon Commission to state that the Nagas should be excluded from the coming political reforms in India, and that Nagas – who were neither Hindu nor Muslim – should not be made part of the Indian union.

1935: Government of India Act 1935 passed. Acting on the recommendations of the Simon Commission, it stated that the Naga Hills District was to be treated as "Excluded Areas," and no Act of the Federal Legislature or Assam Legislature was to apply to the Naga areas. Nagas were the special responsibility of the Governor in the province in his capacity as Crown representative.

1944: Japanese Invasion of India via the Naga Hills. Naga leader, Zapuphizo assisted Subhash Chandra Bose of the Indian National Army and the Japanese army who promised to help Nagas establish self-rule.

1946: The Naga National Council (NNC) was constituted. It grew out of the Naga Hill District Tribal Council, which was an initiative of Charles Pawsey, the Deputy Commissioner of the Naga Hills. In its meeting at Wokha, the NNC declared in its resolution that it stood for the solidarity of the Naga tribes.

1947: NNC memo to Bordoloi's Advisory sub-committee on North East Frontier Tribal Areas and Assam excluded and Partially excluded areas asked for an "Interim government" for a period of ten years and a referendum after that to decide their future. However the talks broke down.

1947: Sir Akbar Hydari, Governor of Assam, made a Nine-Point agreement with the Nagas, known as the Hydari Commission. It provided legislative, judicial and executive powers and protection of lands and resources of the Nagas but there was a disagreement on the ninth clause and the Constituent Assembly would not ratify it.

14th August 1947: Nagas declare independence. Nagas received support of Mahatma Gandhi.

15th August 1947: Hydari Agreement was not accepted and the Naga Areas were constituted as a district under Assam in the new nation of India.

1951: The Naga Plebiscite signed by 99 percent of Nagas for Naga sovereignty was signed and sent to the Prime Minister of India. The Naga Plebiscite was ignored by the Indian government.

1952: First Indian General Elections in Naga Hills. The NNC boycotted the elections so that there were no Naga candidates or voters in the elections.

1953: Assam Maintenance of Public Order Act was passed sanctioning arrests without warrants, imposition of collective fines, and proscribing of public speeches and meetings.

January 1956: Declaration of Naga Hills as a disturbed area under the Naga Hills Disturbed Area Ordinance and Assam Public Order maintenance Act and replacement of the Assam Rifles battalion by the Indian Armed forces took place.

March 1956: NNC forms the Federal Government of Nagaland and hoists the Naga flag.

August 1957: Naga People's Convention held under the chairmanship of Dr Imkongliba, which spoke for the settlement of the Naga problem.

December 1957: Naga Hills Tuensang Area Act provided for a separate administrative unit for the Naga Hills, separate from Assam.

1958: Armed Forces Special Powers Act passed sanctioning search and seize and arrest without warrant and shooting even to the causing of death, with complete protection of the military and paramilitary forces from legal charges.

1963: Nagaland, the sixteenth state of the Indian Union, formed and inaugurated by Indian President Radhakrishnan in Kohima.

6 September 1964: Cease-fire. The Peace Mission constituted of the following members, Rev. Michael Scott, B.P.Chaliha, chief minister of Assam, and Jayaprakash Narayan successfully negotiated a cease-fire between the Government of India and the Naga Underground.

1964: Peace talks begin at Chedema peace camp between the government of India and Nagas, but ends in deadlock. The Peace Mission prepares and presents the 'Peace Mission proposals.'

1975: Shillong Accord signed by the Representatives of Underground organisation and Indian Government stated that the Nagas would accept the Indian constitution. Created great discord in Naga Underground, led to factionalism.

January 31,1980: Breakaway of National Socialist Council of Nagaland (NSCN) from NNC. Led by Isak Swu and Th.Muivah and Khaplang the NSCN was formed and it broke away from the original NNC.

November, 1989: Breakup of NSCN into NSCN Khaplang and NSCN Isak-Muivah.

1997: Ceasefire declared between NSCN (IM) and Government of India and peace talks begun and continued until 2007.

February 2008: Forum for Naga Reconciliation formed, headed by Dr Wati Aier, to reconcile all warring Naga groups. Dialogues with all groups begins.

September 2009: Signing of "Declaration of Commitment" by Underground groups at the Joint Working Group for Naga reconciliation.

APPENDIX II

The Simon Commission

To,

The Indian Statutory Commission,

Camp India

Memorandum of the Naga Hills.

10.1.1929

Original letter dated (26.03.1928)

Sir,

We the undersigned Nagas of the Naga Club at Kohima, who are the only persons at present who can voice for our people have heard with great regret that our Hills is included within the Reformed Scheme of India without our knowledge, but as administration of our hills continued to be in the hands of the British Officers, we did not consider it neccessary to raise any protest in the past. Now, we learn that you have come to India as representatives of the British Government to enquire into the working of the system of Government and the growth of education, and we beg to submit below our view with the prayer that our Hills may be withdrawn from the Reformed Scheme and place it outside the Reforms but directly under the British Government. We never asked for any reforms and we do not wish for any reforms. Before the British Government conquered our country in 1879–1880, we were living in a state of intermittent warfare with the Assamese of the Assam valley to the North and West of our country and the Manipuries to the South. They never conquered us, nor were we ever subjected to their rule. On the other hand, we were always a terror to these people. Our country within the administered area consists of more than eight tribes, quite different from one another with quite different languages which cannot be understood by each other, and there are more tribes outside the administered area which are not known at present. We have no unity among us and it is only the British Government that is holding us together now. Our education at present is poor.

The occupation of our country by the British Government being so recent as 1880, we have had no chance or opportunity to improve in education and though we can boast of two or three graduates of an Indian University in our country, we have not got one yet who is able to represent all our different tribes or master our languages much less one to represent us in any council of a province. Moreover, our population numbering 102,000 is very small in comparison with the plain districts in the province, and any representation that may be allotted to us in the council will be negligible and will have no weight whatever. Our language is quite different from those of the plains and we have no social affinities with Hindus or Muslims. We are looked down upon by the one for our 'beef' and the other for our 'pork' and by both for our want in education which is not due to any fault of ours. Our country is poor and it does not pay for its administrations. Therefore, if it is continued to be placed under the Reformed Scheme we are afraid that new and heavy taxes will have to be imposed on us and when we cannot pay them all our lands will have to be sold and in the long run we shall have no share in the land of our birth and life will not be worth living then.

Though our land at present is within the British territory, the Government have always recognised our private rights in it, but if we are forced to enter the council of the majority, all these rights may be extinguished by unsympathetic council, the majority of whose number is sure to belong to the plain districts. We also much fear the introduction of foreign laws and customs to supersede our own customary laws which we now enjoy. For the above reasons, we pray that the British Government will continue to safeguard our rights against all encroachment from other people who are more advanced than us by withdrawing our country from the Reformed Scheme and placing it directly under its own protection. If the British Government however, want to throw us away, we pray that we should not be thrust to the mercy of the people who could never have conquered us themselves and to whom we were never subjected; but to leave us alone to determine for ourselves as in ancient times. We claim (Not only the members of the Naga Club) to represent all those tribes to which we belong: Angamis, Kacha Nagas, Kukis, Semas, Lothas and Rengmas.

Signed by/-

1. Nihu, Head Interpreter, Angami
2. Hisale, Peshkar, Angami
3. Nisier, Master, Angami
4. Khosa, Doctor, Angami
5. Gepo, Interpreter, Kacha Naga
6. Vipunyu, Potdar, Angami
7. Goyiepra, Treasurer, Angami
8. Ruzhukhrie, Master, Angami
9. Dikhrie, Sub-Overseer, Angami
10. Zapuzhulie, Master, Angami
11. Zepulie, Interpreter, Angami
12. Katsumo, Interpreter, Angami
13. Nuolhoukielie, Clerk, Angami
14. Luzevi, Interpreter, Sema
15. Apamo, Interpreter, Lotha
16. Resilo, Interpreter, Rengma
17. Lengjang, Interpreter, Kuki
18. Nikhriehu, Interpreter, Angami
19. Miakrao, Chaprasi, Angami
20. Levi, Clerk, Kacha Naga

Appendix III
The Plebiscite
A LETTER TO THE PRESIDENT OF INDIA

Naga National Council
Naga Hills, Kohima
To,
The President
Republic of India,
New Delhi.

Your Excellency,
The Naga National Council desires to invite the attention
of the Government of India to the position taken as early
as 14th August 1947, by the people of Nagaland and
subsequenty endorsed by the Naga National Council from
time to time to the effect that Nagaland shall be constituted
into an Independent Sovereign State (separate from the
Union of India) and also the resolution of this same council
dated December 11, 1950, which is to the effect that with a
view to furnishing the people and Government of India with
evidential and conclusive proof of their national aspiration
and for independence, the popular desire of the Naga people
in this behalf shall be presented in a collective verdict of
the adult population of Nagaland which shall be obtained
through the recognised democratic method of plebiscite.

The plebiscite shall be a voluntary plebiscite on the part
of the Naga people and the purpose of holding the same on
a voluntary basis are expressly to remove from the minds of
the people and Government of India any possible difficulty

to accept and recognise the genuinely representative function of the Naga National Council for its nationals in Nagaland, to remove any possible element of doubt as to the passionate desire in the hearts of the Naga people for freedom and independence from India, and lastly but with a genuine feeling of goodwill to avoid any possible injury that may otherwise be done to the reputation of India in the event of a plebiscite held under international auspices should such a reference to the people result in a hundred percent Nagas being in favour of severing governmental connections with India.

A plebiscite such as now being proposed to be voluntarily taken by the Naga people has been brought to a regrettable neccessity by the scant attention paid to the case of the Naga people by the Government of India despite very fervent and earnest pleadings with India for a friendly understanding of the issue.

Throughout these recent years of their direct association with India, the people of Nagaland, while keeping the goal of independence uppermost in their minds, have repeatedly offered to make concessions in order to secure an honourable agreement on a basis which will provide scope for their growth towards full independence while maintaining the most friendly and cordial relations with India. In an attempt to implicate the Naga people in their constitution and thus curb the Naga right to self-determine their own future, India has handled the Naga political issue in a manner contrary to the spirit underlying the pains the Nagas have taken to resolve the difficulties which stood in the way of the parties arriving at an agreed solution. The Naga people had made it clear that recognition by India of Naga right to independence was the basic issue and any arrangement which ignores or runs contrary to this basic issue would be unacceptable to the Nagas. It came as a matter of great surprise, therefore, that India sought to incorporate the Naga territory and coerce Nagaland into a forcible union by the compulsion of a constitution even while the issue of Naga political independence was still under the process of negotiation. However, the people of Nagaland, to whom the question of having a common constitution with India never existed, have made it perfectly clear to the Government of India and their accredited representatives that in so far as Nagas are concerned the Indian Constitution neither affects the status of Nagaland nor alters the basic issue.

The people of Nagaland are keenly aware of the paramount need of India for strong and secure frontiers in this side of her territory and not only are they aware of this, they are anxious to strengthen India's hands to achieve the desired need. It would, however be foolish on the part of India to be deceived into the belief that the Nagas would make their unreserved contribution even at the peril of their national honour and right to freedom. The political independence of Nagaland and the manner in which that independence is to be inaugurated are, therefore, matters of vital importance to both India and Nagaland. Accredited representatives of the Government of India have admitted that if Nagaland should elect to be independent, she has the right to do so. This approach is important as it points the way to reconciling the anxiety of the Government of India for strong frontiers with the Naga case for independence.

The fate of the Free Nagas occupying a country contiguous with Naga Hills and having common boundaries with Burma and China cannot also be betrayed by the British conquest of the Nagas. Of these Nagas India knows nothing except the fact of their existence and their independence. The fact that

Free Nagaland has no international status does not entitle India to incorporate it in her Constitution.

As such, it will be a dastardly act of aggression on the part of India to gratify her inordinate desire for territorial expansion, if Free Nagaland should be ravished. The respect which Burma and China have for the independence of Free Nagaland should be emulated by India as well. We are certain India will benefit by her doing so. That will gain for India the goodwill of the British conquered Nagas too, for sooner or later the now separated Nagas will unite and be free.

So important an announcement as this communication conveys would, under normal conditions deserve to be delivered to Your Excellency in person by a representative of the Naga National Council. That this could not be done has been due to indecent receptions representatives of the Naga people have had the misfortune to experience in the past on a number of occasions at the hands of India's high officers. The Naga National Council could not be certain the Government of India might not again refuse to grant to the representatives to seat an interview with Your Excellency. The Naga delegation which was in Delhi seeking an audience with the last British Governor-General in 1947 and later another Naga Delegation with his successor were persistently prevented from doing so. The Naga delegation sent to Shillong was also similarly denied (by the Government of Assam) a meeting with the first President of the Republic of India. But these incidents, however insulting to our national self-respect, fall into insignificance when it is remembered that the Government of India did not hesitate to use even the army to slaughter the nationals in cold blood.

Another possibility that could not be overlooked was

the Government's habit of arresting Naga political workers while at large in Indian cities – an incident not incapable of repetition. In order, therefore, to avoid similar insults, this commication is being sent to Your Excellency the Governor of Assam who – advisedly – in the words of the Secretary of the Ministry of External Affairs, Government of India, "shall have to be in the full picture."

The plebiscite that will soon take place in Nagaland is intended to reaffirm the position of the Nagas and to bring to India the urgent need of their undertaking the immediate setting up of a Naga Sovereign State. The exact date on which the plebiscite would commence will be announced before long. It is the desire of the Naga National Council that the Government of India will send their observers to witness the plebiscite from beginning to the end. It shall be the privilege of the Naga National Council to give every possible facility to such observers to enable them to achieve their purpose with complete satisfaction.

Yours faithfully

A.Z.Phizo
President
Naga National Council
Kohima
January 1,1951

APPENDIX IV
The Nine point agreement

The Nine Point understanding between Sir Akbar Hydari, Governor of Assam and Naga leaders arrived at in June 1947

1. JUDICIAL: All cases whether civil or criminal arising between Nagas in the Naga Hills will be disposed of by duly constituted Naga Courts according to Naga customary law or such laws as may be introduced with the consent of duly recognised Naga representative organisations; save that where a sentence of transportation or death has been passed there will be a right of appeal to the Governor.

2. EXECUTIVE: The general principle is accepted that what the Naga National Council is prepared to pay for, the Naga National Council should control. This principle will apply equally to the work done as well as the staff employed.

While the District Officer will be appointed at the discretion of the Governor, Sub-Divisions of the Naga Hills should be administered by a Sub-Divisional Council with a full time Executive President paid by the Naga National Council who would be responsible to the District Officer for all matters falling within the latter's responsibility, and to the Naga National Council for all matters falling within their responsibility.

In regard to:

(a) Agriculture – The Naga National Council will exercise all the powers now vested in the District Officer.

(b) C.W.D: The Naga National Council would take over full control.

(c) Education and Forest Department – The Naga National Council is prepared to pay for all the services and staff.

3. LEGISLATIVE: That no laws passed by the Provincial or Central Legislature which would materially affect the terms of this agreement or the religious practices of the Nagas shall have legal force in the Naga Hills without the consent of the Naga National Council. In cases of dispute as to whether any law did so affect this agreement the matter would be rendered by the Naga National Council to the Governor who would then direct that the law in question should not have legal force in the Naga Hills pending the decision of the Central Government.

4 LAND: The land with all its resources in the Naga Hills should not be allocated to a non-Naga without the consent of the Naga National Council.

5. TAXATION: That the Naga National Council will be responsible for the imposition, collection and expenditure of land revenue and house tax and such other taxes as may be imposed by the Naga National Council.

6. BOUNDARIES: That present administrative divisions should be modified so as (1) to bring back into the Naga Hills District all the forests transferred to the Sibsagar and Nowgong Districts in the past, and (2) to bring under one unified administrative unit as far as possible all Nagas. All the areas so included should be within the scope of the present

proposed agreement. No areas should be transferred out of the Naga Hills without the consent of the Naga National Council.

7. ARMS ACT: The Deputy Commissioner will act on the advice of the Naga National Council in accordance with the provisions of the Arms Act.

8. REGULATIONS: The Chin Hills Regulations and the Bengal Eastern Frontier Regulations will remain in force.

9. PERIOD OF AGREEMENT: The Governor of Assam as the Agent of the Government of the Indian Union will have special responsibility for a period of 10 (ten) years to ensure the due observance of this agreement; and at the end of this period the Naga National Council will be asked whether they require the above agreement to be extended for a further period or a new agreement regarding the future of the Naga people arrived at.

APPENDIX V

Historical Rights of the Nagas and their Quest for Integration

Speech by Niketu Iralu*

"All of history can be written in two small words: Challenge and Response." According to British historian Arnold Toynbee, this principle governs the growth of peoples, nations

---

* The best analysis of the struggle: author

and civilizations. We should know this principle governs our struggle also. Our struggle represents our response. The dangerous society we have produced reveals the quality of our response.

How Nagas came to have historical and political rights also tells the story of a people responding to the challenges of a changing world impacting them and compelling them to grow. The response, representing their thinking, grew in intensity in proportion to the increase of the relentless impacts. The thought, a combination of fear, insecurity, aspirations, hope and defiance developed over the years into the fierce Naga struggle for peoplehood and consolidated sovereign nationhood as we know it today. Nagas have all along maintained their struggle was to defend their sovereignty on the basis of their history. It was not a case of Nagas asking for it from anyone.

The Naga memorandum to the British Simon Commission revealed how much Nagas had thought about their identity as a people up to the time of the Commission's visit to Kohima in May 1929. The statement they made became the first written record of what the Naga pioneers at that time had decided was the political right of their people as warranted by the facts of their history. The correspondences between the Nagas and the British from then on consistently and unambiguously reiterated the position they had declared in 1929. The Akbar Hydari-Naga pact, proposed by the then Government of India (GoI) showed the statement by the Nagas to the Commission had been taken note of. The Naga National Council (NNC) declared Naga independence on August 14, 1947, a day before India's declaration, reaffirming what Nagas had stated in 1929, in response to Delhi's unilateral termination of the discussions of the Pact in progress. The Plebiscite of 1951, the total boycott of the first two Indian General Elections, and the all-out, extremely costly fight by the Nagas to defend their declared position, clearly demonstrated how seriously they regarded what they had said. The fight to uphold the Naga position has continued up to this day, notwithstanding the tragic fragmentation of the struggle into the various factions, the biggest one of which is the State of Nagaland as it is today.

We cannot really blame the GoI for the stand it has taken all along with regard to the issue of Naga sovereignty. India has simply defended the integrity of the map she inherited from the British. Any other government in its place would have done the same thing. But Nagas too cannot be blamed for insisting that they had made their position categorically clear before the British left their empire in South Asia. The British invaded their land; the Nagas fought against the invasion, and were defeated. So when the British were leaving Nagas declared their right to decide their own future, and they fought heroically to uphold that right. Nagas therefore were not, are not, secessionists because they did not break an undertaking for union they had made with India before the British left. They are not anti-India 'hostiles' or irresponsible trouble-makers, as they are often impatiently called by bureaucrats who have not read the records, and repeated by the media without knowing the facts. Nagas regard themselves as honourable neighbours of India. They know they are extremely small and weak, but they expect mighty India to respect them, their history and their struggle to defend its facts and honour, as King Porus of old did with Alexander. It should be stated that India has started to understand.

Right from the beginning of the Naga struggle it was always clear that it was for the entire homeland of the Nagas. In fact, this is Article No.1 of the Yezabo. No Naga was thought or said to be excluded from the purview of the Article. Then when Nagaland State was created, the State Assembly passed three unanimous resolutions reaffirming what had been stated in the 16-point Agreement on the coming of all Nagas under one administrative roof.

I should digress here a bit to point out that perhaps a priceless opportunity to settle the question of integration was missed when Nagaland State was being created. It has become almost as tough as sovereignty today, as far as Delhi is concerned. Those who went to Delhi and accepted Statehood should have told Nehru that they risked their reputation in the minds of their people and their lives to come to Delhi to study his proposal, and so they could not, would not, go back without integration being agreed to by Delhi which they could tell their people and those sacrificing their lives for Naga rights. If they had taken this firm stand, integration of all the Naga inhabited areas would have been part of the settlement. The creation of the State was so important strategically for Delhi to suppress the Naga freedom fighters, Pandit Nehru would have phoned the Assam Cabinet of the day and the authorities in Shillong controlling Manipur and NEFA on behalf of Delhi, and his command would have prevailed. Nehru was so powerful at that time it was inconceivable his instruction would have been disobeyed. And by so acting as instructed those obeying him in Shillong and Imphal wouldn't have been doing anything unjust to anyone because any area not part of the ancestral homeland of the Nagas did not need to be part of the proposed Nagaland.

The creators of the State rushed back home to start the formation of the State, and no doubt to swiftly fill up the chairs of power that became available. The rush was unseemly and what they failed to solve then because of the rush has turned out to be extremely costly. We too would most probably have done just as they did if we were in their places.

To come back to my subject, it has become clear that NSCN-IM has run into what the NNC and its FGN ran into earlier during the negotiations with Delhi following the cease-fire of 1964, namely, that Delhi is in no position at all to talk on sovereignty, not because the Naga case is wrong or legally and politically invalid, but because India is too young a democracy still in a chaotic state of formation to handle the issue. And Nagas have done virtually nothing to speak to the minds and hearts of the Indian people whose understanding alone can solve the problem. We have talked only to a succession of politicians in Delhi whose minds are too distracted to listen sufficiently to us to understand the facts of our historical and legal position. The politicians have left our memorandums to junior bureaucrats to keep in their neat files to be referred to only when necessary occasionally. We must know that the junior bureaucrats who have kept our files are seldom above the rank of Deputy Secretary in the obscure North East section of the Union Home Ministry in Delhi. The Indians who have implemented Delhi's position are the various branches of the security forces of India and the Ministers and bureaucrats in the Planning Commission. We cannot be proud of what the Planning Commission has to say about the Nagas. The Indian people do not know the facts of our history.

Nagas should have long ago gone to the Indian people, to get them to understand why we maintain our position is unique and why we are not secessionists. This would have kept us united, kept our struggle alive, focused and healthy because we would be getting the most important audience for us in the world to understand us. By going outside India we got the uninformed Indian public to needlessly suspect us and react against us, reducing ourselves to being treated by Delhi with its hated carrot and stick policy only. Alas, we have learnt to tolerate the stick but become pathetically addicted to the carrot! We should learn from this costly mistake.

How much I had wished Phizo had left London and come to India soon after he found the British were in no position to help us no matter their emotional feelings for us, coming from the support Nagas gave them during the second World War, because they couldn't afford to lose the huge Indian economic market. If he had landed in Delhi and declared he had come to discuss with the great people of India and with his own people in Nagaland, he would most probably have been taken straight to Tihar Jail. Perhaps not? But the Naga struggle would then have been transformed, made clean, dynamic and relevant again. The battlefield would then have shifted from the jungles and villages of Nagaland to the teeming cities and towns of the whole of India, perhaps at first through Tihar Jail? There were indications that he started to think that way, but before he could work out the formidable logistics he passed away, isolated, misinformed, therefore distrustful of others, more than was wise, and heart-broken. Adinno has continued to stay on in London needlessly isolated, seriously misinformed and saying things some of which, according to me, are unwarranted, too personal and too divisive. I understand her compulsions. Her sacrifice, which I believe all respect, qualifies her to be a healer in our history.

The time has come when Nagas must reach a settlement with India which will consolidate what we have achieved so far and enable our people to grow together on the consolidated foundation. It is clear Nagaland will not be a member of the UNO as a sovereign republic following the envisaged settlement. But the settlement will be right, honourable and acceptable to Nagas if Delhi will sign it by acknowledging the Naga struggle is not a secessionist struggle because, unlike some of their neighbours who also started their 'liberation' struggles and fronts, Nagas had made their position abundantly clear long before the British left. If Nagas are prepared to negotiate for something other than sovereignty despite the full legal legitimacy of their claim for it, because they understood India's difficulty on the issue, it should be not too difficult for Delhi to accept what Nagas mean by 'honourable, acceptable settlement.' It will be right and just for both sides. If needed Nagas should go to the people of India to ask them to understand the facts behind our stand and create the needed public opinion that will enable their government in Delhi to act.

I believe, what is required is all the rival factions sitting down together to work out the precise terms for a negotiated settlement with Delhi that will be honourable. Let it be not sovereignty, but an interim settlement, leaving it to the future generations to decide what will be best for them according to their best judgment in their time.

As for integration, we should know that Delhi will keep on saying it is not possible. What else can Delhi say or do? It is too risky for any party ruling in Delhi to disturb the status quo in Assam, Imphal or Arunachal. Our mistake has been overestimating ourselves and underestimating our neighbours, and the complicated implications of the integration issue. We have too arrogantly shown our position to be that once we reach a settlement with Delhi, Delhi will force Manipur, Assam and Arunachal governments to accept integration of Naga areas. This has been a serious error, showing we have not realized the crucial reality that our neighbours too have now woken up, and on many issues they are far more awake and proactive than us.

We should tell Delhi we fully appreciate and understand Delhi's difficulties on integration also, and that the question should be left to the neighbours involved to work out a solution that would be fair and acceptable to all sides. The idea will work if neighbours will go to one another as neighbours should do. There are signs that the neighbours are now ready to do this for the sake of achieving a common stability for the good of all.

We must go to the people of Assam, Manipur and Arunachal to start serious, honest conversations with them. Let them know we are more interested in first listening to them to understand their difficulties, fears and paramount needs than in finding solutions right away. This will create the atmosphere of trust that will enable listening to one another possible to evolve the solution all can accept as fair and honourable.

A needless blunder has been describing the issue of integration as one of creating a Greater Nagaland/lim. Nagaland is Nagaland, nothing more and nothing less. Our careless talk of a Greater Nagaland has raised doubts and fears in the minds of our neighbours that we are thinking of claiming lands not part of the ancestral homeland of the Nagas to be part of the envisaged settlement.

The doctrine of life for living on this planet of ours which we have not examined sufficiently is one of our fundamental failures that has rendered our struggle unpursuable and too destructive. I'll try to explain what I mean.

Henry Ford pioneered the modern mass production process that profoundly affected the pace of industrial productivity and economic development in general. The hundreds and thousands of cars that rolled out of the Ford Motor Company in Detroit, Michigan, were painted black. Ford's standing instruction was that the cars could be painted in any colour 'provided it is black'!

I think we can say God is also somewhat eccentric and arbitrary like Ford when it comes to how life on earth is to be lived including how we pursue our struggles to grow.

God seems to allow everything, even the most horrible things. Can we deny He doesn't solve problems on His own although it is true He acts to solve them the moment we cooperate with Him. He seems to be happy with all our professions, our political, economic, religious, cultural and other pursuits. He seems to say, 'Do all you are inspired to do, provided what you do will help the building of my kingdom on earth as it is in heaven.'

We can say he allows us to fight and struggle for our political aspirations and dreams as people and nations. He even seems to allow the coming into being of all our political factions! He certainly hasn't stopped them. But can we deny He is saying to us that our struggle should contribute towards the building of His kingdom on earth, the just society in Nagaland where we care for one another, enable one another to do their best and be the great people He means each community, each individual to be? We know the hell we have created by struggling in our own ways to achieve our aspirations, saying politics should be done that way.

I believe when the struggle was started, as in the struggles of almost all peoples, our leaders had not thought enough to know that even if the goal may be right and noble, if the method adopted to achieve it is not clean or morally and ethically right, the method destroys the struggle and the people eventually. This doctrine of Ends and Means made famous by Mahatma Gandhi was the oposite of the doctrine of the left and the right that said 'If the goal is good do anything even if wrong to achieve the goal.' We need not go into what adopting wrong methods to achieve what is good and noble has done to the world.

The pioneers in Phizo's time who battled together did a monumental job in defining the identity of their people. Although the issues they confronted had not become as complicated as they have become today, the price paid by them and the people of the day was also extremely high. They were taking the first steps of their people's journey into the unknown. It was a single focus struggle to establish the political position of the Nagas. They did it and gave their people a priceless heritage.

But as the struggle progressed it ran into the inescapabale moral and ethical issues that are at the heart of all human struggles. When disagreements arose due to genuine doubts and apprehensions that always occur in all great ventures, the dissenting voices were condemned as threats to the cause which led to the first killings of Nagas by Nagas. By and large the reactions to these killings were contained because the movement had not fragmented yet, and Nagas were confronting something they had not thought much about.

But the mental, spiritual traumas and the physical pains caused by the wounds were real. The questions raised by them marked the beginning of the real crisis of the Naga struggle because the NNC leaders could not ignore what had been revealed, namely, that there was more to non-violence than they had thought and declared to be their policy. This is not easily said with any self-righteous condenmnation of our pioneer nation builders. For, if I were courageous and capable enough to be in their places, I too would most likely have supported, condoned or rationalized the killings 'under the political circumstances.' To raise the doctrine of Ends and Means at this perilous time of our crisis is hazardous because it is likely to be misunderstood. But to ignore it is to deprive ourselves of the only chance of working our way forward together in a new way that will work.

The truth is during the earlier stages, the crisis over the killings did not make news mainly because of the reasons mentioned earlier, and the rebuke of conscience to respect life was still whispering loudly from inside. But gradually the heavy pressure compulsions of personal and 'national' interests 'to achieve the goal' that always drive a political struggle took over. The unorganized killings that began as a matter of course during the early stages of the struggle were quietly rationalized and justified to be inevitable in politics. In more recent years, insensitive, blasphemous justifications started to accompany killings. The killings of the latter period thus became more known and more condemned. In addition, use of violence and threats to collect money, remove obstacles out of the way, mislead people, etc, 'for the national cause and principle,' came to be loudly justified over the last decades. Those who use less or covert violence may argue that their sins are less serious because it was true the scale of Nagas killing one another was much less during the early stages. But this argument does not get any one of us far with God.

Did God make a mistake in making Nagas into so many tribes? And did He make a second mistake by giving them a common desire to be a people and a nation? We know God makes no mistakes. So it must be that He has given us a very tough assignment and that is to learn to live together by giving our best to one another, not our worst, preferring one another 'to make the other person great.' He wants us to give this secret to countless peoples in our neighbourhood and beyond who confront the same problems and needs. Our struggle is God's plan for our growth wherein we change wherever needed.

'To live is to grow. To grow is to change. To grow fully is to change often' (John Henry Cardinal Newman)